Cops and Hitmen

Stuart Thompson Mystery Seires

RJ Beam

Disclaimer

This is a work of fiction. Names, characters, businesses, places, events, locales, and incidents are either the products of the author's imagination or used in a fictitious manner. Any resemblance to actual persons, living or dead, or actual events is purely coincidental

Other Works By RJ Beam

Stuart Thompson Mystery Series

Fire Cop (book 1)

Cops and Stalkers (book 2)

Cops and Hitmen (book 3)

Stand Alone Books

Final Thoughts

Anthologies with a Short Story by RJ

Perspectives, Volume I: An Emergency Medicine and Public Safety Anthology

After Midnight: Tales from the Graveyard Shift

Chapter One

"The thing about college parties is, if they are not bothering anyone, why bother them?" Officer Thompson was trying to explain to his trainee the finer points of local police politics.

"Okay, but underage drinking seems to be a major problem here. Back when I was a student it seemed like people got busted every week."

"Back when you were in college, you mean last week?" Stu could not help but crack a joke at the expense of his new protégé. "This campus has close to nine thousand students. How many underage drinking tickets did you read about in the student paper each week?"

"I don't know. Maybe like ten."

Dana Walker was the daughter of State Fire Marshal John Walker. A man Stuart Thompson had the pleasure of solving a few interesting cases with. Now, Stu was showing young Officer Walker the ropes as a city cop. Sometimes the world seemed tiny. "Fairly small percentage if you do the math... right?"

The two officers were walking the sidewalks around the fraternity houses of the University of Wisconsin Platteville. Thursday nights for some college kids were the start of the weekend. Parties on Thursdays were rather common. On the streets surrounding the campus, it was easy to pick out the Greek society houses from general off-campus housing; the frats kept up appearances. Mowed lawns, flower beds and generally nice landscaping. Although the Greek letters bolted to the siding also gave it away.

Pointing at a house, Dana said, "Look, all the other houses on the block have lights on. This one is basically dark. I bet they have the windows covered. You can pick out hints of light at the edges of a few windows. You know they are having a party. Blacked out the windows so no one can see inside."

"Very true, but listen." Stu put his hand to his ear for effect. "Nothing. Maybe a hint of some music in the air, but it could be coming from any house around us."

"So we should investigate. That is the job of the police, to investigate crimes."

"Ah, but let me ask you this. If there is no victim, do we have a crime?"

Young Officer Walker seemed stumped at first. "Yeah but, we arrest drunk drivers all the time and they haven't hurt anyone."

"True, but they have the potential to. Plus, traffic law is way different from status crimes, like underage drinking." Stu looked at the house, then back at the rookie cop. "How many cars do you see parked on the street here?"

"A couple. Why?"

"If they were having a party, don't you think there would be more cars?"

"Well, they must do something smart, like providing a sober person to taxi people to and from the party."

Thompson snapped his fingers. "Exactly."

"I don't get it."

"Why should we fear young people drinking heavily when underage at a party?"

"They get out of control. Someone is bound to drive home and have a crash."

Stu pointed at the house and the street. "Is anyone out of control at this place? How likely is it that someone will crash when drunk leaving here? You said that the hosts are likely to provide rides. Also, the dorms are close, so a lot of party goers are likely to just walk."

"So what you are saying is a party is not a police problem until someone is dumb and makes it into a problem."

"As one training officer I had once called it 'people being stupid in a no-stupid zone' until we got folks calling nine-one-one. We leave these guys alone."

Officer Walker was still in her first week on the job. This was only her third day in uniform. Thompson did not enjoy training officers in their first week. Young officers were always so black and white, with no perception of the gray area created by police discretion. Textbooks and academy time can't teach someone about political winds and community priorities related to how laws are enforced. The academy taught officers what the law was. Out on the street, they would learn when or if laws were enforced.

If given his choice, Thompson enjoyed getting new officers in the third phase or the fourth phase of the training program. By phase three, rookie officers had been working the streets for six weeks. At that point, a rookie had confidence and was open to learning the advancement of their skills. They filled the first weeks with hand holding and correcting mistakes. Thompson did not like the facet of training that involved telling someone everything they did was wrong. He enjoyed having someone who did well and used positive reinforcement to take their skill to the next level.

"So what you are saying is, even though we are on foot patrol in a high party area, you will not let me bust any parties."

"Yes, and no... I am going to teach you to respond to a complaint from someone who feels negatively affected by a party. But in the current political climate, we don't go looking for parties. Good job on spotting all the clues about the fact that the house is hosting one. For now, just file that information away to use if later someone calls in a complaint."

The rookie officer looked dejected. Thompson could tell the young woman was itching to make an arrest. It was true of many new police officers. Their chief priority was making arrests, forgetting many other aspects of police work. Nuances that textbooks and lectures by Criminal Justice professors just did not convey.

Feeling he needs to toss the kid a bone, "Listen, it is still early. The bars are not busy yet. How about we make it a priority to do some bar checks tonight? Find someone underage with a fake ID in the bar."

"Now you have me all confused. Why is a party okay but a fake ID card not?"

Thompson cracked a smile. "Good question. A fake ID is a fraud. Not to mention, many people heading to the bars are driving. The party houses are all close to dorms, but not the bars."

The two cops walked the sidewalks of Main Street with Officer Thompson pointing out important locations for the younger officer to be aware of. Besides the Fraternities and Sororities houses, the rental homes that acted as unofficial dorms for various sports teams.

A middle-aged man walking towards them interrupted their discussion. Graying hair, still fit and trim, but dressed in clothes about ten years out of date. Stu barely paid the man any attention. Officer Walker stopped and seemed to stare at the guy. It took a second for Thompson to realize his recruit had an interest in the older guy.

"Niente"

"Hey man, what did you just say?" Dana Walker was showing some initiative by contacting the man.

The man had passed by Officer Walker. "Scusami... err... I sorry officer. I talk at myself." He had stopped, turned to face the cops and held his hands up mid chest, palms out.

Thompson figured the kid had never met one of Platteville's more eccentric residents. "Hi Bob, delightful night for a walk."

"Yes nice. Am I under the arrest or can I go free?"

Before Stu could say anything, Dana blurts out. "Is there a reason we should arrest you?"

"No, no officer. I sorry. Can I go free?"

"Bob, I would like you to meet our newest officer, Dana Walker. Dana, this is, well ah, this is Bob."

Officer Walker reached out a hand for a handshake. "Got a last name there, Bob?"

Bob looked at the officer's hand. He didn't reach for it. "I know rights. I did not answer questions unless I got the lawyer here."

Thompson put a hand on Walker's shoulder, a nonverbal signal to back down. "I am just out showing the new officer some of the hot spots around campus. Not looking for any arrests tonight, it is her first week. Just tour guide time."

"Good... you honest cop Mr. Thompson. You never hassle me like others. You have safe night, okay?"

Thompson thanked Bob, and the man continued walking the path he had been on before the encounter. Walker watched the man till he turned the corner on Elm Street and cleared from view. "That was weird."

"Yeah, guess I should have warned you about Bob. He is a local legend, for lack of a better term." Thompson laughed, thinking about his first time meeting Bob. It went about like how Dana's encounter just went. "Dude has lived here about thirty years, from what I have been told. Almost everyday he walks around town. Every so often, he gets on the Greyhound bus and leaves town for a week."

"His accent was kind of thick. What was that Italian? So what's his story?"

"No clue about his story. He just walks around. Never gets in trouble, so no clue what his real name is. Someone called him Bob and the name just stuck. Must have some mental issue or something because he asks about being arrested all the time, yet he seems to be a choir boy and does nothing wrong."

"Maybe he is some kind of sovereign citizen. That is their mantra 'am I being detained'. With that accent, English could be his second language, so detainment is mixed up with arrest."

Stu looked in the direction the man vanished off. "I doubt it. He never pulls any of the other rhetoric of the sovereign citizens. I think he is just a lost soul and hates sitting home all day."

Before Dana could respond, the radio speakers on both their shoulders called out, "Platteville to all city officers. Report of a fight in the parking lot of Draft Shack liquor store."

The officers were only three blocks from the Draft Shack. Turning around, Stu could see a group of people in the parking lot. Dana looked at the senior officer as if seeking permission to head towards the fight. Nodding at the younger cop, Stu said, "make sure to tell dispatch we are close by and going to take this call."

"P38 to Platteville, myself and P27 have eyes on the fight. Mark us out on that call."

"Ten-Four."

Stu started a light jog towards the scene. No need to run. The dispatcher had not indicated any weapons were being used. Dana jogged along a few steps ahead of Stu. It was obvious the rookie wanted to run full out at the fight scene. She had not learned yet how exhausting a physical confrontation could be. Trying to fight a suspect after running was even worse. No, Stu set the pace at a jog, so they still had the energy to physically subdue suspects if needed.

When they reached the scene, there was a loose circle of five people watching two guys rolling around on the ground. One guy pinned the other and raised his fist. Stu reached them in time to grab the raised fist. "Police officer! Stop fighting."

While still holding the fist in his right hand, Stu slid his left hand down to the suspect's raised elbow. With a slight pivot, Stu had the suspect in an arm bar lock. Stepping in close caused the suspect to move off the person on his back and, with just a hint of pressure, Stu had the suspect lying facedown on the asphalt.

Stealing a glance at the onlookers, Stu yelled, "Everyone needs to take about ten steps back from me." Two people had cell phones out, recording the incident. "Record me all you want but move, NOW!" The circle of people all moved back.

In a quick practiced motion, Stu got the suspect cuffed and then watched as Dana cuffed the guy who had been on his back. Sitting the two guys up, it was obvious both had landed punches on each other. Each had some facial bruising and hints of blood at the nostrils.

"Okay boys, care to tell me what this fight was all about?"

No one said a word. When asked about medical aid, both refused. Officer Thompson then decided to walk both men back to the police department and cite both for disorderly conduct. As they stood up, Stu noticed Bob was at the end of the block watching. He seemed to smile and nod at Stu, almost like an appreciation of how he dealt with the fight.

Chapter Two

Stu was standing on a ladder taping, and mudding newly hung drywall. The bluetooth speaker on the floor belted out classic rock from a streaming service. Singing along, Stu was enjoying feeling as if he was accomplishing something.

He had a police radio sitting on a sawhorse on the side of the room. Listening in to the goings on like some civilians do on police scanners. Although as a volunteer firefighter, having the scanner gave Stu a few extra seconds of warning before his pager went off.

"Platteville to P23."

"This is P23."

"Please respond to 720 E Mason Street for a barking dog complaint. Caller reports the dog has been howling nonstop all afternoon. Sounds like this is an ongoing problem at this address."

"Roger that, on my way."

Nuance calls were a bane for many police officers. Thefts, injuries and dead people are easy to deal with. Unhappy neighbors always take way more time than anyone assumes they should. Laughing to himself, Stu was happy to have a Saturday off.

Lately, a weekend off for Stu Thompson rarely gave him actual down time. His home was a hundred-year-old Victorian on Main Street just a few blocks outside the downtown business district. Just four months earlier, Thompson's girlfriend had died in his living room on New Year's Eve. A serial rapist murdered her.

A few weeks later, the rapist got caught. Because of a conflict of interest, Stu was not overly involved in catching the criminal. However, an informant provided Stu with a key piece of evidence that allowed the suspect to be identified.

For years, Thompson wanted to gut and redo some rooms in the house. His girlfriend's death gave him a reason to. He was also reconfiguring some walls and the arrangement of rooms. What had once been the formal dining room and office was becoming a huge greatroom. The former living room was split in half to add a new main floor bathroom and make a smaller office space.

By changing the configuration, the room Christina died in no longer existed. It had been unnecessary to do so, but Stu went as far as to remove the subflooring in the former living room. He wanted to remove any trace of that former crime scene.

Upstairs, Stu was also making changes. What had been a four-bedroom house was now only going to be a three-bedroom home. He was expanding the master bedroom to add an on suite bathroom and walk-in closet.

At first, after Christina's death, Stu wanted to sell the house. Talking to a real-estate broker, he found out the market for his home would be minimal. Also, anything he looked at was way smaller or too far out of his price range. Ultimately, remodeling was the most logical choice.

Working with his hands gave him purpose. Power tools and proper measurements kept Stu away from alcohol. It was slow work doing it all himself, but the longer the job took the longer he would be busy. He was almost done and wondered if he was going to be okay.

Thoughts of Christina were less often, but the emptiness was still there. Once the work on his house was done, Stu wondered if the thoughts of his lost lover would come back. He created some profiles on various dating sites. He even downloaded the Tinder app to his phone. So far, no one captured his mind like Christina had.

"P23 to Platteville".

"Go for P23."

"I am in the neighborhood and do not hear any barking dogs. Put a note on the door of the suspected address with a warning about the complaint. Mark me 10-8." Stu had to set down his mudding trowel as he laughed about the call on the radio. Typical day shift nonsense. Someone was upset over noise, but as soon as the police arrived, the noise was gone. It was one more reason Stu kept on the night shift as long as he had.

Once the humor passed, Stu was back up on his ladder, mudding up the drywall. The work was mindless, easy to just escape into the tunes coming from the speaker. Nothing to think about. Just work the compound around to create an even surface between the sheets of plasterboard.

As he worked, Stu lost track of time singing along to KISS and AC/DC. His ear perked up as the police radio squawked out, "Platteville to all city cars and campus units. Report of a car versus pedestrian crash at Broadway and Mineral Streets. Unknown injuries at this time. Will try to get more information from the caller."

Stuart's home was just a block away. His house was on the corner of Broadway and Main Street; Mineral Street was the next road north.

Dropping his tools, Stu jumped off the ladder. He grabbed the police radio from the charging base and headed for the door leading to his driveway.

Outside, he paused for a second, looking up the street. A few cars were stopped at the intersection. People were milling about, but he could not tell what was going on. Jogging up the block, Stu kept his eyes and ears open for information about what had happened.

Laying in the roadway, three citizens surrounded a man. Two had their cell phones out, taking photos. One man stood back with his hand over his mouth. Stu guessed the guy keeping back was the driver of the car who hit the person lying in the roadway.

As Stu got closer, he realized who the hurt person was. It was Bob. He must have been out on one of his daily walks.

Approaching the victim, Stu asked Bob where he was hurt. Bob's eyes had a wild, unfocused look in them and his feet were twitching.

"Bob, it's me, Officer Thompson. I am here to help. Where are you feeling pain?"

His eyes remained unfocused. Bob said nothing, nor even turned his head to the sound of Stu's voice.

Kneeling down, Stu set his radio on the road and took hold of Bob's head. He held Bob so there could be no movement in the neck, causing paralysis. Stu then asked a bystander to pick up his radio and help him communicate with the dispatcher.

"P27 to Platteville."

"Go ahead 27" the dispatcher had more of a questioning tone in her voice. Stu guessed she was wondering why an off-duty cop was on the radio.

"I am on the scene of the crash on Broadway Street. Patient is semi-conscious, not responding to questions. No major visible injuries besides a few scrapes on his arms and his head. Holding C-Spine till EMS gets on scene."

Sirens in the background alerted Stu that help would be on scene soon. Dispatch reaffirmed that "10-4, you should have an officer there any moment and EMS will be on scene in two minutes."

When the first squad car reached the corner, Stu breathed a sigh of relief. Kneeling in the road had left him exposed to being hit by a car, as well. Visions of a kid texting while driving and hitting him had flashed in Stu's mind within seconds of touching Bob's head.

Two other squad cars were right behind the first. Sergeant Eli Noris approached Stu with a medical bag. "How is he?"

"Not sure. Think he might have smacked his head hard on the roadway. He is totally out of it."

"What should I do?" As usual, because Stu was a volunteer firefighter, everyone assumed he had advanced medical training. In Platteville, the ambulance service and the fire department were two unique entities. In some cities, the two are joint services, but not everywhere. As such, Stu had about the same medical training as all his fellow cops.

"I have him. Can you deal with the guy there in the gray shirt? I think he was the driver who caused this."

Sergeant Noris seemed relieved as he walked away from Stu. The sound of the Ambulance siren grew closer. Kneeling on the asphalt was hurting Stu's knees. His back was sore from being bent over. It had only been two minutes since he started holding Bob's head, but it felt like an hour.

When EMS arrived, a medic Stu knew as Shawn got out and came over first. Stu saw two other medics jump out of the vehicle and start pulling equipment from compartments. Shawn squatted next to Bob. "So, what's the story here?"

"Car versus pedestrian crash. Male victim with unknown extent of injuries. No visible major bleeds. Minor scrapes on arms and head. Has massively altered alertness. Not responding to any questions, nor is he making any communications."

Stu could see Shawn eyeing him up. He imagined the EMT was questioning why the officer was not in uniform. "Are you involved in the crash or just passed by and stopped to help?"

"No, I live at the other end of the block. Overheard the call on my radio and felt compelled to come out."

"Cool. Give me a second to feel for any deformations on his skull and then we should be able to take over all the patient care from you." Shawn felt around Bob's head. His arms worked around Stu's arms like a roadside game of twister.

The other two medics made their way over with a gurney and other assorted medical gear bags. One was placing a hard plastic board on the ground while the other was opening the plastic bag on a neck collar. After the medics got set, Stu helped as they transitioned Bob onto the board. Then, after the neck collar got secured around Bob's neck, Stu slid his hands away.

Standing up, Stu's legs and back ached. Shaking out the stiffness, he made sure the EMTs no longer needed his help. Satisfied his help was done, Stu left them to their patient. Stu then got the attention of Sgt. Noris. "Do you need anything from me, or can I go home?"

"That depends. Did you witness anything or just come out to render medical care?"

"Nope, didn't see a thing. Came out after hearing the call and jumped right into doing first aid."

"Okay, you better still do up a report and have it in the file. No need to mess up your day off to come do it. Just make sure it gets done next time you are in."

"Sounds good."

Back in his living room, Stu stood looking at the ladder. He suddenly felt unmotivated to keep working. Stomach growling told him he needed to eat. Random thoughts made him want a beer. Wants versus needs was a constant battle of will. Once again, his will won out as Stu walked back to the kitchen for food and not a beer.

Purposefully, he kept no alcohol at home. A weekend bender followed by a monster hangover caused him to dump anything remaining in the home down the drain. Over three months later, sobriety caused Stu's body to change. He had always been athletic and trim. Extra calories from drinking made it so he never had defined muscles. Not that he was a heavy drinker, but still, even a few drinks a week were empty calories his body did not need.

Lately, he had noticed he was actually sporting six-pack abs. With summer coming up, Stu was thinking he might make sure to do some lawn work shirtless. A trip to the beach might be in his summer plans as well. Maybe come summer he will be ready for a rebound type hookup. A ripped torso could help to have someone desire him only for his body, in a short-term aspect.

A sliced chicken breast, some vegetables and a spoon full of canned peanut sauce went into a pan. Into the microwave went a bag of rice. Once the meal was ready, Stu sat at his kitchen counter. A little Asian inspired stir fry and scrolling social media on his phone. A typical single guy lunch.

Lunch didn't provide any motivation to get back to mudding the drywall. A trailer video online made Stu remember he had yet to see the new blockbuster superhero movie. It felt like a good day to take a break. Seeing a movie would be a pleasant change. Going shopping that did not involve home remodeling materials also sounded good.

After putting his plate in the dishwasher, Stu was just about to head upstairs to change when his phone rang.

Chapter Three

"Hello, this is Stu." He did not recognize the number on the caller ID screen.

"Sorry to bug you again on your off day, but we have a little problem." The voice on the other end of the phone was Sgt. Noris. "Do you know Bob's real name?"

"No, why?"

"The folks down at the ER need to know. Sounds like he needs some surgery and they want to get into contact with his family."

Stu thought about any interactions he had with Bob. He had never actually had any official contact with the guy. "Wish I could help, but I have only ever known him as Bob. Don't think I have ever even had a call where he was a witness or victim. Do we have anything on the in-house database on him?"

"No. I even called a few of the older retired officers, thinking they might know. Nothing."

"Hate to ask a stupid question, but did the ER staff check all his pockets for identification?"

"Yep, I am actually at the ER calling you on the phone in the exam room. I checked everything. All he had was a few bucks in cash in a paper clip."

"Is he from town? Can we contact people from the schools to find out what happened to his family?"

There was a pause of silence from Sgt. Noris's side of the phone. "I don't think so. From what I understand, he showed up in town a couple of decades ago. Never had an actual job, always lived in an apartment over the jewelry store on main street. Called the building owner. Even he has no records. Bob pays cash for rent. Owner inherited Bob from the previous owner. There was no paperwork or renter application on file. Because Bob pays in cash and is always early with rent, the guy never thought to ask for anything to be filled out."

Stu paused to think. "Want me to come in and roll his prints? We might never have arrested him, but someone could have. Maybe he spent time in the military. Heck, the guy has an accent and an odd way of talking. Maybe he hails from some other country. If his prints are on file, I could find out and put a name on him."

"It is funny you would offer to do that. Now I don't feel bad asking you to come in."

The two men enjoyed a little chuckle before Stu hung up.

Christina had been an ER nurse. Stu had known her from stopping out at the hospital on shift. They didn't start dating till the two had a class together while working on their Master's in Adult Education degree. A group project had them doing homework at Stu's house.

Their homework turned into a sleepover. Which eventually turned into a solid romance.

In the months after her death, Officer Thompson avoided the hospital if possible. As an Officer In Charge (OIC) on the night shift, he could have the junior officers on shift take calls in the ER. Walking through the doors to the emergency room made Stu wish he was not such a proficient evidence technician.

Armed with a black leather folio he had picked up at the police station, Stu approached the nurses' desk. A cute blonde with purple streaks in her hair looked at him with a questioned face. Pulling a badge hanging on a chain out of his tee shirt, Stu asked where Bob was.

"Oh, sorry officer. He is in exam room three." She pointed out the way to the room. Thompson indicated he spent enough time in the ER to know the way. "I thought I had met all the cops. Just started in February. Lisa, by the way." She held out her hand.

Feeling obligated, Stu took her hand. "Stu. Nice to meet you, Lisa." He then excused himself to go get his assigned task done.

Entering the exam room, he saw Sgt. Noris and Dr. Sherbahn talking. The men turned, and the Sergeant thanked Stu for coming in.

"The CT scan showed a depressed skull fracture. It is a fairly minor one, but we still need to get him into surgery to lift the bone fragments to prevent anything from damaging brain tissue."

Stu was perplexed. "This is an emergency situation, right? You can do this without consent. Why the urgency to find some family for him?"

"Good question." Dr. Sherbahn smiled at Stu. Christina always enjoyed working with Dr. Sherbahn and Stu had developed a respect for the man as well. "Because he has not woken up. Yes, this is emergency surgery. So we don't need loads of consent forms signed. However, we need to know about advanced life-saving directives and organ donation."

"Ah... got it. You need to know about life support or not."

"Exactly."

Opening the leather folio, Stu pulled out the tools. As he worked, the three men talked about sports and movies. The folio had a selection of metal trays shaped like crescent moons. Each one was wider than the other. It also held strips of paper and an ink pad.

Holding a tray up to Bob's fingers, Stu checked to see if it was the proper size. Happy with his selection, Thompson loaded a strip of paper into the slot on the tray. He then took the ink pad and gently tapped it on each of Bob's fingers. He then pressed each finger into the paper on the tray.

Satisfied with the results, Stu excused himself and returned to the Platteville Police station.

Back in the police's basement department, Stu turned on a computer recently installed in the evidence workroom. On it was a program called AFIX Tracker. This program could connect to the FBI fingerprint databases and produce matches for people in the system.

While the FBI had created the Automated Fingerprint Identification System (AFIS) to match fingerprints. The computer matches don't exactly hold up in court. Meaning a person still needed to compare prints after the computer match. AFIX, a private company, created a product small local departments could use to help speed up the process before submitting prints to the experts at the crime lab to make the final match.

Stu would never testify in court about the fingerprints he matched with this AFIX system. However, he could use it to narrow down an investigation to a smaller pool of suspects. Or with Bob, try to see if he could put a name to an otherwise John Doe body.

Using the system was fairly straightforward. He scanned the prints into the computer. Imputed a case number and his badge number. Then Stu clicked on the search icon. Knowing the search could take hours, Stu walked upstairs to see who was around.

The open concept cubicle farm used by officers for a work area was vacant. Along the far wall, all the doors leading to the department administrator's offices were closed. It made sense the administration rarely worked on weekends.

Strolling into the dispatch center, Stu found the lone call taker sitting at his desk. From listening to the radio at home, he already knew who was on duty. Carl, a college kid who worked part-time doing dispatching. Stu found Carl annoying. It was not so much that Carl was a bad person; he was just too enthusiastic.

Carl was only twenty years old. He still had pimples on his face and often came to work dressed in sweatpants and a polo. The dispatch center had no dress code, as the public would rarely ever see a dispatcher. Unofficially, the chief made it known he wanted dispatchers in collared shirts. Most people understood collared shirts also equaled work pants. In his youthfulness Carl seemed to think that sweatpants were okay.

The television was on, turned to an old action movie on some cable channel. Carl was so transfixed by the movie he didn't notice Stu walking in. "What ya' watching there?"

"Huh?"

"I recognize the actors and know I saw this once, but can't place the name. What movie is this?"

Carl looked at Stu, hiding his surprise that someone else had come into the room. "Not sure what the title is. Was channel surfing and just kind of stopped on it."

The two sat in silence for a few minutes, watching the mindless violence on the television. Poor dubbing had all the lead actors' swear words covered over by appropriate television words in a slightly different voice. In Stu's mind, the use of the coverup word called more attention to the fact they had said a curse. Better to just let it be said than hide it.

Finally, a commercial came on. Carl looked at Stu. "Why are you in here, anyhow?"

"Victim from the car crash is that guy who walks around town. No one knows his name, and he did not have an ID on him."

"Oh, you're talking about Bob, right?"

"Yep."

"Yeah, I heard he is some kind of retired spy from the CIA or NSA."

Of all the rumors about Bob that Stu had been told, this was about the stupidest. "I doubt it. Most likely he is just some guy who grew up with a massive trust fund and decided he hated big city social scene life. Moved out here to be anonymous and enjoy a simple life worry free."

"Not what I hear."

"You're still a kid. You'll believe anything. Think about it. With just a few million bucks, you could live here in Platteville for a lifetime paying cheap rent and an easy-going college town lifestyle."

The commercial break ended, and Stu turned to watch the movie. Not so much that he was into the movie. More, he just did not feel like debating if Bob was a world-class spy or not. When the next commercial came up, Thompson excused himself from the dispatch center and returned to the basement.

The AFIX system had a message on the screen about a potential match being made. On television, it always looked like a computer did all the work. In real life, the computer gave potential matches and a human made the final assessment. Thompson felt excited that he was right to run Bob's prints in the system.

Stu had always imagined Bob was some rich person who ran away from the trappings of society life. Moving to Platteville was an escape from drinking and drugs. A substance abuse related charge was what Stu was thinking Bob would be on file for.

Clicking on the message window, Stu opened the match screen. Checking over the pattern, Stu saw the print found was a bunch of circles, otherwise known as a whorl. Bob had whorls on a few fingers and his left thumb. After inspecting the print on the screen, Stu guessed by the size it might be a thumb.

Fingerprints have many multiple landmarks. Places where the ridge lines end, split into two lines or where two lines cross each other. Stu worked to identify a group of landmarks and matched each one between Bob and the potential match. Over the course of the next hour, Stu matched up fifteen unique points. The print in the computer must belong to Bob.

A few more clicks and Stu pulled up a menu, asking to identify the person in the match.

UNKNOWN SUSPECT

Punching the desk, Stu let out a growl in frustration. How could there be a print on file but no name?

After requesting the system to show details, Stu figured out that there was no name. This print was not connected with a full set of fingerprints on file. It was a single thumb print recovered at a crime scene.

Digging deeper into the details, the thumbprint had been at two crime scenes. Both crime scenes from the St. Louis area. Homicide cases with no suspect, just a thumb print that was not associated with a known suspect, till today.

Chapter Four

Detective Greg Massana cursed himself for wearing a long sleeve shirt and pullover windbreaker. April in Chicago was always a crap shoot related to weather. One day it can be sunny with decent temperatures, the next nearly freezing with rain. Earlier in the week it had been cooler, but the temperatures were inching into the mid-sixties.

Greg was eating a gyro from a favorite food truck. Museum Park was filled with people enjoying the pleasant temperatures. A good number of the folks had on professional clothing. Office workers out getting some sunshine on their lunchtime. Some, Greg guessed, were playing hooky. Putting a "meeting" on their calendar, then go off to chill over a long meal break.

A few kids were in the park as well. Likely skipping out on school. If he was a uniform officer, maybe he would go make contact. But as a detective he was not concerned with such trivial issues as kids cutting class.

Two women in yoga pants and sports bras came walking up the sidewalk. Their bodies shapely yet fit. Housewives who subscribed to the 'strong is the new sexy' mantra. Greg tried not to stare, but could not help it. He found a strong-looking woman to be attractive.

One lady glared at him with a look of disgust. He must have been a tad obvious: he was leering. He said an internal curse at himself for being a creeper. As they passed, the other lady gave him a smile. Then her eyes widened. She must have seen the Chicago PD logo embroidery on his windbreaker. As they continued down the path, she looked over her shoulder back at him twice.

They had that look of living in the neighborhood close to Michigan Avenue close to the park. Jet black hair, good curves and tight-looking ass. The lady who smiled was exactly his type. If she came from money, it made her even more attractive. If she lived close, this might be a regular walk for her. Maybe Greg will have lunch here again. Try to meet her.

A buzzing in his pocket alerted him to an incoming email. It was from a rarely used Ymail account. The app was set to buzz but not make any noises. It was a personal email. Greg did not want fellow officers asking if they heard the announcement tone.

Checking the email, it took him back for a second. It was an automated alert a friend at the state department of justice had set up for him. Someone had checked in on a John Doe warrant in the national system.

Skimming the details, Greg realized he needed to act quickly. Someone in Wisconsin had loaded a fingerprint into the system that matched an unknown suspect from Saint Louis. He did not know why this unknown suspect was important, but they had paid him to keep alert if someone accessed the file. They did not pay him to ask questions about why he was just given cash to funnel information on the down low.

Alfonso's Pizza was not known for being one of the best places in town to get pie. It had a close following in the neighborhood it occupied. The dining area was smallish, but they did a brisk takeout and delivery business. Greg imagined they sold enough pies to cover the cost of the business without needing the alternative income the place also received.

Stepping inside, the aroma of garlic and sausages made Greg hungry. His gyro had filled him, but that homemade aroma made the mouth water. He made his way across the dining room nodding a hello to the man standing behind the bar dominating the left side of the dining room. Three older guys sat at the bar. They were always at the bar on the same stools. None of them looked directly at Greg, but all three were looking in the mirror behind the bar, eyeing him up.

Passing into the kitchen at the rear of the restaurant, a cook looked up to see who was coming into their space. Almost as quickly as he looked up, the cook had his head down again, putting sauce onto a crust. Greg passed the cooks without a word. Turning to the right he wound around some prep areas in the kitchen to a door frame.

Inside the door was a stairwell both going up to the second floor and down to the basement. Greg had never been to the basement but knew it held the walking freezer and cooler needed to run a restaurant like this. Rumor had it the basement held two walk-in freezers, one for food and one for the building owner to keep other "items" cool.

At the second floor landing, two men the size of NFL linemen stood in silence. One had a buzz cut, the other a long ponytail. Both had pistols tucked into their waistbands in direct violation of Chicago's gun free zone laws. Looking at them, Greg knew breaking gun laws was the least of the criminal activities they had been involved in.

"I need to talk to Mr. DeRege."

The two guys glanced at each other, then back at Greg. "He is not expecting you today," they said in unison.

"Yeah, I know. Something came up that he needs to know about right away."

Buzz Cut nodded his head. "Things come up sometimes. I can take a message and pass it on."

Frustrated by organizational hierarchy, "don't think that will work. I need to know what he wants me to do. This could be time sensitive."

"Lots of people say they have important information for the boss. Often it is a waste of time, stuff he already knows."

"Think about who I work for. When I have time sensitive info, it is not some dumb tweaker mouthing off about rumors. Mr. DeRege pays me for my access to inside information that snitches on the street could not get."

Ponytail gave Buzz Cut a slight nod then opened the door to the apartment. Motioning for Greg to follow. Ponytail walked him to the kitchen area. "Have a seat. The boss is taking a little after-lunch siesta. He should be out in less than half an hour. Don't go no place or touch anything till he comes out."

Greg watched the pony tail dude make his way back out to the top of the staircase landing. Glancing around, Greg surveyed the apartment he had been in many times before.

Mr. DeRege actually lived out in the suburbs, but spent much of his time in this apartment. He owned the building and his cousin, Alfonso, owned the pizzeria down stairs. It was a two-bedroom unit with one bedroom set up as an office. Greg had been in the office many times, but never in the bedroom. The kitchen served as the unofficial waiting room for anyone seeking a meeting with DeRege.

Out in the living room sat a plush black leather sofa and hung a massive seventy inch flat screen television that Greg could not recall ever seeing used.

Looking out the window, Greg watched the people going about their lives. He sat nervously, contemplating how his message would be received. The temptation was to pull out his phone and play a game or scroll over posts on social media. If DeRege saw a phone out, he might assume Greg was recording the conversation, making his life expectancy brutally short.

Ten minutes after sitting down the bedroom door opened and two young women sauntered out. There was no way they were ever over twenty-one, but Greg assumed they were likely right around nineteen. Short skirts, v-neck tops and impractically tall heels, good odds they were working girls. They both smiled and waved at Greg. He nodded a reply as they wordlessly walked to the exit.

Five minutes later Anthony DeRege came out of the bedroom. "Greg!" If he was surprised to see the cop he hid it well with a tone of friendly exuberance. "Where have you been hiding? I haven't seen you in weeks."

"Been busy. Street gangs having open season on each other here in town."

"I know, each week the paper gives the tally of the number shot and killed over the weekend. Makes me want to think about getting into the gun selling business, ya' know."

"Makes me want to think about moving out to the suburbs where being a cop is a lot less dangerous."

"Yes, you looked stressed. You should have let me know you were coming by today. I could have had a third girl here. A mid day blowjob keeps the body healthy and mind clear."

Greg could not help but to laugh at how the guard called it a nap, yet the boss was blunt about getting his dick sucked. Anthony DeRege was the guy who told it like it was, yet also never allowed others to disrespect him by speaking honestly behind his back. It was a trap of power. "A blowjob sounds good, but I am here to talk about something important."

"Oh..." Pointing at the door, "You want, I could call them back up here? We can talk and then after you get your rocks off."

"No, not today. As much as it pains me to say so."

Mr. DeRege took a seat at the kitchen table. "Okay detective, what do you got that is so important today?"

"I got an email alert about someone accessing a John Doe warrant."

Confusion crossed DeRege's face. "What's a John Doe warrant?"

"Ah, sorry... when we have evidence in a case to link a suspect to a scene but no way to identify the suspect we can still create an arrest warrant. Because we don't have a name, we list the warrant as a John Doe. This way, if we ever link someone to the evidence the cops can hold them."

"How can you have evidence but not link a person? I don't get it."

"Say we have fingerprints or DNA at a crime scene. If the suspect was never arrested, their profile is not in the system. Sometimes, if it is important enough, we leave the file open, hoping the person will at some point be booked into a jail."

"But why need a warrant? If they book the person into the clink, you know where to go get them, right?"

"You assume they are being booked for a crime. What if a guy gets a simple drunk driving arrest? Hooked up on a Friday night and kicked loose on Saturday morning. By the time the paperwork gets done up on Monday, he has skipped town, knowing he narrowly avoided prison. Put a warrant in the system and the dude gets held till he goes in front of the judge."

"Enough with the police lessons. What does this John Doe guy have to do with me?"

"You asked me to check a couple of cases out of St. Louis a few years back. I got a friend at the state records office to flag the case in the system and email me if someone accessed it."

Anthony looked out the window. "Go on."

"Some cop up in Wisconsin ran a set of prints and got a hit off the warrant. Other than that I don't know much."

Sitting forward in his chair Anthony asked, "Where in Wisconsin?"

Greg had to pull his phone out and look at the email. "The terminal is identified as belonging to Platteville. No other details about why the print was run."

"Shit-" Anthony looked out the window, then at his watch. "Looks like you are taking a little road trip, detective."

"Wait... what?"

"I know who the John Doe is. I need you to find out why the cops ran his prints. Depending on the situation I might want him back here in Chicago, otherwise you need to make sure he can't talk to anyone, ever."

"There is no way I can take a trip to Wisconsin. Don't you have anyone else that can do this?"

"I told you once what you will be doing. Figure out a way to make it happen. Don't make me repeat my order. Do I make myself clear?"

Chapter Five

"This is Investigator Mike Radvich."

"Hey Mike, this is officer Stu Thompson from the City of Platteville, Wisconsin, calling. Ran some prints today and got a hit on a John Doe warrant from your agency."

"Whoa no way, brother. Got a case number?"

Stu had to shake his head. He had never gotten into the whole calling fellow cops, brother. When some folks said it, they sounded fake. This Mike guy had a jovial tone of voice. Stu imagined this officer truly did view everyone working in police work as a brother. "Yeah, when I called your central info line I gave the case number to the girl and she connected me to you." Stu then read off the case number to Mike.

A low whistle came across the phone. "Holy shit, brother. You got this guy in custody or you find his prints at a scene like us?"

"We have him in the hospital."

"No way... This is one Grade A bad ass mother fucker you got. Any cops get hurt taking him down? You guys shoot him or what?"

"No, nothing like that. Car crash. No identification, so we did prints before surgery. Doctors wanted to know about organ donor status just in case."

There was a pause on the other end of the phone before Mike said. "So you have no clue who this guy is?"

"None was hoping you could help us out?" Stu could not believe someone was calling Bob a badass.

"Damn brother. To be honest, we got no clue who he was except some kind of ghost. Killed multiple members of the Nino family. Gutted them with a knife and left the knife behind like a calling card. At two scenes, we got a print off the knife. Some of the mafia task force folks say there are a dozen hits of both Mafia dudes and bikers around the Midwest with the same MO."

"There is no way Bob is some kind of psychotic killer. This has got to be some kind of error."

"Hey now, hold on. Who is Bob? You said you didn't have an ID on the guy in your hospital."

Stu took a few minutes to fill Mike in on Bob walking the streets of Platteville for years. While every cop in town would say Bob was a few fries short of a happy meal, a heartless killer was not a thought they would hold. He was so unassuming and seemed so introverted.

"Well dude, I think this Bob guy was playing you. Hiding in plain sight. Sorry to be ignorant, but how big is your city? You got much for organized family or biker activity there?"

Stu felt a bit embarrassed, saying he was in a college town. "Just over ten thousand full-time residents and a college of ten thousand more people. We are not Mayberry, but crime here is not very organized. Unless you count a few rednecks pooling resources to cook meth out at the trailer court."

"Don't know what to tell you. His prints were on the knives he left behind at the scenes. Unless he was a knife salesman who sold the weapons to a killer. I find that doubtful, so you got yourself a hard-core killer in your hospital."

"So did you work on these murders or you are just the unlucky guy who gets to take the calls from out-of-town cops?"

"I am a member of our organized crime task force. We don't have a strong mafia family here, but the Nino family runs a lot of the drugs, mostly heroin, and prostitution in the area. They own a few bars and some strip clubs. Believe it or not they even have a film studio where they make semi amateur porn movies. Because the dead guys are from the Nino family, yeah, they assigned me as part of the case."

The two cops chatted about what Stu knew about Bob. Mike told Stu more details about the crimes they suspected Bob was involved in. After about twenty minutes, Mike said. "It has been good talking with you brother, but I need to talk to my boss about you guys having this Bob dude in custody. If we send some officers up that way, would you be our contact?"

"Maybe. My boss does not know about this identification yet. Wanted to contact you guys and find out as much as possible, so when he asked questions I had answers."

"I like the way you think, my brother. Okay, write my cell number down. And if you would be so kind, give me your direct contact." Mike and Stu then exchanged numbers and hung up.

Sgt. Noris was sitting at the nurses' station in the emergency room when Stu came in. The Sergeant had taken the laptop from his squad car inside the hospital and was typing away on it. Stu assumed he was catching up on paperwork.

Looking up from the computer screen. "Did you find anything?"

"Yeah, but you will not believe it."

"He is the long-lost heir to the Hilton or Kardashian family?"

"Try Murder suspect. Got a warrant on him for two murders and details from the case tie him to about a dozen more."

Sgt. Noris let out a long whistle. "You're joking... right?"

"Nope. Just got off the phone with a detective from St. Louis. Bob kills by knife. Buries the knife in the gut and leaves it there. Twice thumb prints were left on the knife."

"Seriously? Don't fuck with me, not in the mood right now. Don't tell me this guy is some kind of serial killer."

Stu stood silent for a few seconds. He was unsure how to broach the topic. The man who killed Stu's girlfriend, Christina, had been a serial rapist. When sex was not enough thrill, the guy turned to killing. Technically, the suspect in that case had crossed the threshold to serial killer. The college town was still reeling from his crimes. Stu knew a second serial criminal could be a disaster for the city.

Finally Stu said, "Well, you see the people he allegedly killed are all involved in organized crime. Mostly mob and a few biker gang members."

"What-?"

"Yeah, that was what I said. It looks like Bob is some kind of hitman."

While Stu talked to the hospital staff about not having an identity for Bob, Sgt. Noris called the police chief. Less than a half hour later, Chief Ruiz was at the hospital asking for the officers to fill him in on everything they knew.

Bob was in surgery and after would get moved to an intensive care recovery room. Hospital staff had said the injury looked to be only the skull fracture, so no need to rush Bob to Madison for invasive brain surgery. After they set the skull, Bob would likely be asleep for a few more hours. Pain medication might keep him incoherent for a day.

The Chief sat at the nurses' station in blue jeans and a black polo shirt. Stu silently wondered if the chief had changed before coming into the hospital. Appearances seemed to be important to the Ruiz. He always dressed semi formally. He was not the chief who wore the uniform regularly. Typically, he was in a shirt and tie.

The chief came to Platteville from the New York state police. He had been a high-ranking administrator in NY running an investigations division. After retirement, Ruiz looked for a job as a smaller town chief in Wisconsin to be closer to where his son and grandchildren lived. He was drawing a pension from his old job and a nice paycheck from the new city.

"So you are telling me we have zero ID on this guy, but he is suspect in a bunch of killings?"

Stu hated to say it, but he said, "Correct. His prints come back to two crime scenes. The style of the kills is a lot like a few other scenes. So the organized crime task force guy I talked to thinks they linked him to all the deaths."

"Okay, now fill me in how every cop in town seems to know this guy as Bob, yet we don't know who the fuck he is."

Sgt. Noris took over for Stu. "He is just some average citizen. Never had police contact."

"What do we know about him?" The Chief asked.

"He came to town a few decades ago. Lives above the jewelry store on Main street. Everyone sees him walking the streets of town daily. He does not seem to interact with any people unless required to. Clerk at the grocery store, waitress at the diner and that is about it. Any time a cop tries to chat him up he asked if he is being detained. Basically, all the guys decided to ignore him. Crazy guy walking the sidewalks endlessly."

Chief Ruiz paused before saying. "Every town has that one odd person."

"Best we can tell he does not have a job. Urban legend is he was some kind of rich trust fund kid. Some folks think he moved here because the family kicked him out for being crazy. Other folks think he moved here to get away from bad influences of parties and drugs."

"Wait, if he walks the streets here every day how did his fingerprints make it to crime scenes in Missouri?"

"Every so often he goes on vacation. We would see him walking with a duffle bag to the campus student center. Apparently, he buys a Greyhound bus ticket and hops the bus out of town. Few days later, we see him walking back to his apartment with the duffle bag again. Then back to his normal walking the streets."

"I first got into investigations towards the end of the big five families' run of power out east. Didn't exactly work too much of the mafia stuff but had a few cases involving guys who were mobbed up. There were always rumors about the families having ghosts as hitmen. People from out of town who had little connection to the organization. An easy way to keep some extra distance between the family and a killing."

"Chief are you thinking that our guy Bob is the Midwest version of the IceMan?" Noris's eye got wide.

Stu butted in asking, "Who is the IceMan?"

Ruiz said, "There was a notorious killer nicknamed the IceMan. He was a Polish guy so the mafia would not make him an official made man. He lived out in the suburbs of New Jersey. Family and neighbors all thought he was a dull office drone working for some warehouse company. Turns out he was a Grade A hardcore killer. While he was a suspect in about two hundred and fifty deaths, there was only evidence to convict him of five."

Eli Noris added, "There was a movie about him put out a few years back. I am sure it was mostly fiction, but still it showed this guy lived a double life. Imagine what it would be like to hide half your life from people."

"Yeah," Stu said, "I could see how someone would rather live in a small town solo than try to keep a secret like that from a family. Still, Bob just does not look like a cold-blooded killer."

"What does a killer look like?"

"Good point chief. Sorry for saying that."

"I was not admonishing you. Just pointing out you can't judge a book by the cover."

Stu and Eli continued to tell the police chief stories about various encounters with Bob. Cops sitting around telling tales. Eventually, the conversation drew to a natural end. The Chief asked what the next steps were to find out who Bob was.

"When he wakes up we could ask him." Stu said.

"What if he refuses to answer?"

"Sounded like a crew from St. Louis was going to come up and collect him. Guess it is their problem, not our problem. If he wants to go to prison without a name, who cares... right?"

Chapter Six

Sunday afternoon and Stu was back in at the police department. His weekend off had turned into a weekend working. Extra money from overtime pay would go to paying down the loan on his remodeling project. He had spent much of the morning on the phone with officers from St. Louis.

The detectives he had talked to were very interested in learning as much about Bob as they could. They too ended up making a comparison between Bob and the IceMan. Hiding in plain sight.

At the end of their discussion, they decided a detective from St. Louis would come up to Platteville on Monday. Stu was starting the paperwork to get warrants for Bob's apartment. Once the out-of-state investigator arrived, they could check out Bob's place together.

Sgt. Noris came into the officer's work area at the police station. "What are you here for? Go home and enjoy your day off."

"Detective Radvich from St. Louis wanted to talk. He had some of his supervisors who wanted more information about what we had up here. Didn't feel like talking to them at home, so came in here to use the office line."

"Gotcha. Looks like you are off the phone. Why ya' still hanging around?"

"Need to get my report typed up and an affidavit for a warrant started. They got a guy coming up here tomorrow. Hoping if we go into Bob's apartment we can find something telling us who he is. Phone bill, magazine subscription, there has to be something with his real name on it."

"I remember when I was your training officer. You were a total shit magnet. First five minutes we were in the squad car together we got a call about a shooting. I worked here years before I saw someone who had been shot. But you... it only took five minutes of being a cop."

"Well, yeah, but remember that guy shot himself. He was screwing around trying to twirl the gun old west cowboy style. Ended up discharging the weapon. So it was not like that was a real honest shooting call."

"True, it was not a real shooting. However, the way dispatch called it out, it sure as hell sounded like a real shooting. You totally had a look of 'what the fuck am I getting into' on your face."

"Well, to be honest I likely thought that. I remember one thing that flashed in my brain was how I assumed Platteville was a safe little town. You know, nothing ever happens here. Then get called to a shot fired. As we pulled up to the house, a part of me thought it might be rookie hazing. Send me on a hot call to see how I reacted."

Sgt. Noris tilted his head sideways. "Wait, you assumed we were messing with you?"

"Yeah, some of my classmates in the academy talked about stories and legends of pranks pulled on new cops. I was sure it would be some kind of prank. Imagine my surprise to walk in and find a guy laying on his bedroom floor with a gaping hole in his leg."

"All I can say is you did well on that call. First days with a rookie can always be scary. Not sure how they will be when things go sideways. After that call, I knew I could trust you to have my back."

"Thanks Eli... that means a lot."

"Hey speaking of rookies. How is Walker working out?"

"Dana is doing good. Very eager to find self initiated field activity. Sometimes I feel she is disappointed when I tell her we need to slow down."

"Yeah, that is a good problem to have. Trying to get an overly motivated person to work at a healthy pace is much better than trying to encourage an unmotivated employee to be normal." Sergeant Noris then commented about allowing Stu to get his work done. He then walked away, heading towards the exit leading to the squad cars.

Staring at the computer screen, Stu no longer saw the words. Proof reading was not a major strong point for him. In a world where lawyers nitpick any minor detail, looking for loopholes to get their clients off, Stu needed to make sure his documents were error free. Last thing he wanted to do was mess up a case from some other jurisdiction with a typo.

Leaning back in his chair, he felt the report was as good as it would get. Multiple other people would read this before a defense attorney would ever see it. Someone would alert him to an error that was likely still hidden in the text.

"Officer Thompson, if you are still in the building, come to dispatch." Stu rarely hears the building's public address system used. Then again, nearly everybody on duty wore a radio.

It must have been a sign it was time to save his document and log off the computer. He then made his way to the dispatch center. "Hey Carl, what's up?"

"Hospital called. Bob is awake."

"Okay. So... why you need me in here?"

"We got a part-time deputy from the Sheriff's patrol up at the hospital standing guard on him. Deputy called saying Bob has questions, but the deputy has no clue what the answers are. Apparently, Bob told the deputy to get a city cop up there and listed off the names of a few officers he will talk with."

"Let me guess, I am one cop Bob will talk to."

"Yep."

"Why the hell would that crazy old guy want to talk to me versus whoever is on shift?"

"I wondered that myself. But he had a short list of names and none of them were working today. You are in doing paper work. So I guess you get a few more hours of overtime today."

Stu grunted a reply and walked out to the hallway.

Exiting the elevator, Stu shook his head, looking at the part-time deputy. Likely a college kid from the University trying to get some experience on the resume before graduation. His uniform, a size too big, hung from his scrawny frame. Stu knew the kid had to be twenty-one years old because of policy, but he looked younger than eighteen.

A quick flash of his wallet badge and the kid opened the door to the hospital room. The city police did not have a jail. Only the Grant county sheriff's department had a jail, thus Bob was under guard of a deputy. One who had not inspected Stu's badge well.

I could have had a plastic toy badge, and that kid would have let me in. Hopefully, Bob does not have friends who come looking to help him escape.

Rooms in Platteville Medical Center were all single occupancy. Besides the bed, the room had a small couch sitting under the window and a television mounted to the wall. Bob was sitting up in bed with an air tube in his nose, IV in his left arm and some wires going under his shirt to a heart monitor. He picked up his hand and pointed towards his left, at the couch.

Sitting Stu asked "How you feeling? The nurses taking good care of you?"

"This is why I ask to see you. You know how to treat people. Other cops, not so much. You one of the good one. I respect good men. I feel like a truck hit me, not just a car. However, cute nurses come in and I forget the pain for a few moments."

Amused Stu said. "I was a bit surprised you know who I am. We don't talk much."

"I am trained observer. I read your name tag. Know who you is. Remember you. Any time we meet you good and talk. Never make rude words. Never make me feel angry."

"Yeah here's the thing. You know who I am, but we don't know your name."

"Ah... but don't you all call me Bob?"

Stu felt a moment of shame. "Not knowing what else to call you someone just decided to use that name and it stuck. Do you mind if I ask your real name?"

"Libertino Bosso"

"Mind if I just stick to Bob?"

"Haha... ouch... it hurts to laugh. Please don't make the jokes."

Stu stifled a laugh. "Sorry. Didn't think it would be as funny as it came out sounding."

"No is not your fault. People think I am crazy so I never let on that I am not. You first man to crack joke like that to me in many years."

"Seriously," Stu said, "Don't you have any friends?"

"No, not exactly."

Stu felt like he was building a rapport with Bob, or Libertino, whoever he was. A good police interview starts with establishing a relationship. On television, the cops nearly always play tough-guy with someone they are interviewing. Many seasoned officers know acting tough will just cause the other person to clam up. Officer Thompson has never considered himself a great interviewer. He rather works with physical evidence, allowing others to pull information out from people.

"You have lived here for decades. You must have some friends. Every day, you walk around town. Are you telling me you never stop to chat with anyone?"

"Si, yes. No peoples talks at me much. Sure, peoples says the 'hi'. But maybe I never the talk to others, so you know is okay."

"Why doesn't anyone ever talk to you?"

"Officer Thompson, you never make the talk at me. Excuse me if I asks why?"

"I guess there was never a reason to."

"And?"

Stu could not help but to look down at the floor. "People said you were a little off in the head. Not sure if it was crazy or just someone very eccentric."

"So you no like talking to crazy man?"

A little defensive. "As a police officer, we deal with folks that are unstable all the time. If they are not harming anyone, leaving them alone can be best. Just the mere presence of a uniform officer can cause some people to get upset."

"Ah… so you assume if you no bug me I no bug the nice people of the city."

"When you put it that way it makes it sound bad. Why would others think you are crazy? You could not have gotten that reputation overnight moving to town."

"When I moved to Platteville, I speak very little English. I was alone in a strange town. When eating at the diner I could not order food, only grunt and point at food on table next to me. When I took daily walks some people say 'hi'. I said 'hi' back. Then they ask questions I do not understand. So I just shrug or say 'no thanks you.'

Eventually, people stopped saying too much. They think I crazy or how you say… brain damage. At the diner they know to see me what my usuals are. Waitress, no need to talk. Just ask if I want the normal and I nod.

I think maybe someone says something to police once. Asked if it was safe to have crazy man walking the streets. Officer Luker stopped to talk once. He no longer an officer I think, no see him for a long time."

"Yep, he retired back at Christmas," Stu said.

"Officer Luker, he was known as lazy cop. I just smile and nod my head at him. He stopped talking for a minute seemed to be wondering what to say. So I ask him 'am I under arrest?' He tells me I am not so I says 'okay cold out I need to go now' and walked away. He rolls up car window and drives away. I think he thought like you say. Don't bug the crazy guy and he will not go, how you say... go postal"

"Alright, so Libertino what's your story? Why do you want to talk to me today?"

"That kid in hall. He talk to much. Think he can impress nurse. He thinks he get nurse to go home and make love. Can tell she no care for him, yet he talk and talk. I hear him say you found my fingerprints at crime scenes. Think maybe I killed a man or two. Yes?"

"Yes, we found your fingerprints in the computer. I rolled your prints hoping to identify you and notify your family you were hurt."

"But instead you find out I am hitman."

Chapter Seven

Greg Massana was packing his bag. He hoped his brief trip to Platteville would be quick. Get there, find out what Anthony wanted to know about this guy on the John Doe warrant and then get home. As with many things in Police work, nothing goes as hoped or planned for. He packed for four days. If this trip took any longer, he would have to figure out what to wear for clothes.

There are people working in criminal justice who think detectives get weekends off. Problem was crimes happen seven days a week. On television, it might look good to have detectives working Monday to Friday; out in the real world many work rotating schedules much like a patrol officer. Greg, as a junior detective, got stuck working more weekends than not.

He did not mind working weekends. Getting out of his shift to travel was the problem. With the weather, nice people were outside more. Shootings in Chicago were way up. Given a forecast for a sunny Sunday today was bound to be busy.

After his meeting with Anthony DeRege, Greg was called to the scene of a drive by shooting. No one killed, but an eight-year-old had got hit in the arm. An innocent person playing outside in the yard next to the house targeted by the shooters. While on scene, Greg talked about his stomach cramping up. Told his co-workers lunch was not agreeing with him.

The captain commented that her kids had been sick with the flu the week before. She said something was going around with lots of other kids missing school. Other officers joked he needed to eat better, stop hitting the food trucks daily. No matter what they thought he had planted the seed.

"Hey Captain this is Greg," he said into his cell phone. "I don't think I can make it in today. Was up half the night puking my guts out."

"You were looking a little green yesterday. Like I said there is a flu ravaging my kids' class at his school. Wondering when I am going to end up getting it."

"Trust me boss, you do not want to get this. I feel like death."

The Captain's voice took on a motherly care tone. "Are you okay at home alone? Do you need anything? I could see if a squad car can run you over anything."

"No boss. Thanks for the offer. I just want to sleep."

"Okay, get better." The phone clicked off.

Greg almost felt bad for calling in sick. His Captain was always good to him. When she offered to have a squad car run supplies over to him she was fully serious. She would contact the patrol supervisor and make some uniform run errands for her sick detective. The funny thing was a patrol officer would actually view a special assignment like that as a bonus. Helping a fellow cop was cake work compared to taking calls from dispatch.

Sunday would have been his last day working. In cop speak, it was his Friday. Monday and Tuesday were his off days, and Wednesday was his scheduled day to return to duty. Three days, but he packed for four. If he was not home by Wednesday morning, calling in sick would be hard. Officers out sick too long need a doctor's note to verify they were not using sick time for extra vacation time.

Loading his bag into his car, Greg cursed himself for allowing life to spiral out of control like this. He had been young and allowed his dick to override his brain. It was well known that flashing a badge avoided paying the cover charge at most clubs. Including strip clubs. There were lots of young cops who would hit the titty bars on nights off. It was an occasional indulgence of young hot shots.

His downfall happened when Greg transferred from third shift to second shift, three in the afternoon till eleven at night. They staffed second shift with a boatload of cops in their early 30s, many recently divorced. Greg, still in his early twenties, got caught up with these veteran officers who like to work hard, then party harder.

She was a bartender at a club called The Chicago Bush Company. Ironically named given how little hair any dancer seemed to have. Summer was the name she used. Even though Summer never danced on the stage, she still used a fake name while working. Because she was not a dancer Greg accepted when she offered her phone number one night. The next day, the guys on shift kept egging him on to call her.

With veteran co-workers he looked up to prodding him Greg felt it was safe to call Summer. They made a date for a few nights later. Their date comprised going out to eat and a plan to hit a few bars. After eating, she said how working in the bars makes her hate social- izing in them. She then invited him to her place for some drinks.

Having drinks at her place was like a scene out of a porn movie. Within minutes of sitting on the couch, they were both naked. The next day he received an email telling him to come to Alfonso's Pizza. Attached to the email was a photo of him with summer on her couch. An obvious screen capture from a video.

It was the first time Greg met Anthony. The mob boss made a rude comment about how the video of the two fucking was so hot he had jerked off watching it. Then told Greg how he had video of him talking to Summer at the Bush Company. "It would be a shame if these videos got sent to the boys working internal affairs," Anthony had said. And just like that, Greg became a crooked cop, on the take for the DeRege family.

Working for Anthony was not all that bad. He paid Greg, in cash, for services rendered. It was mostly just keeping Anthony informed on police operations. If investigators were looking at someone working for DeRege, Greg would send an alert. This allowed the mobsters to create airtight alibis for their people well before cops came asking questions.

He also acted as a funnel of fake information into the police force. Typically, inside information on DeRege's enemies. Information that helped make arrests of people in competition with Anthony's business interests. Greg enjoyed feeding the police information that helped get criminals off the streets. Although he needed to ignore how it helped the DeRege family grow.

Funneling information into the PD had led to Greg making detective young. Supervisors assumed he had cultivated some good informants as a patrol officer. The assumption was if Greg did such good work in uniform, he would excel in a plain clothes role.

The drive across northern Illinois on I90 was uneventful. Traffic getting out of town and past O'Hare airport had been mild. Now that he was between Schaumburg and Rockford traffic was light. The interstate would soon give way to Highway Twenty. Greg looked at the gas gauge and saw he was just under half full. A rumble in his gut told him getting a bite to eat would be appropriate.

After crossing the city of Rockford, Greg pulled into a chain gas station. Standing between his car and the pump, Greg searched in his wallet. He couldn't charge expenses on this trip to his normal credit card. This needed to be paid for out of the cash Anthony gave him. Cash Greg put into a prepaid Visa.

Trying to be smart Greg was not like other crooked cops. He lived within his means. Small apartment, normal cop clothes, and no fancy car. Most of his cash from the DeRege family went into a safe deposit box. Some he took to a local pharmacy chain to recharge the prepaid credit card he carried. His side income paid for nice meals, upgrades on vacation, and other expenses that were not public in nature.

With his car refilled, and a bag of chips on his lap Greg pulled back onto the highway. According to the GPS, he was about halfway too little old Platteville, WI. He did not recall details of the trip, but he knew his family had taken a drive to Platteville years ago. His dad wanted to see the Bears during their summer training camp. In the early 1980s up to the mid-2000s, multiple NFL teams hosted summer training camps at colleges in Wisconsin.

Greg's dad had been a diehard fan. Going to the college town to watch practice was better than going to a game. Fans were up close to the team. During breaks, players seemed happy to come sign autographs and pose for photos.

The GPS told him the trip would be faster if in Warren IL he turned north and finished his trip on Wisconsin Highways. He had a stop to make first outside of Galena, IL. So he would drive highway twenty across the north of the state for the next hour.

Joey DeRege lived close to the tourist town of Galena. A picturesque city set on the bluffs overlooking the Galena River, just a few miles west of the great Mississippi River. Vacation homes, bed and breakfasts, along with a historic downtown main street, made it a popular getaway spot for affluent Chicago natives.

The DeRege family had a cottage just outside the city on a wooded lot. Located off a narrow back road well away from any regularly traveled roads, it afforded the family an escape for a real vacation. Any Law Enforcement doing surveillance would stick out like a sore thumb on the winding path heading out to the house. Anthony had said many times being out in the woods was the only time he felt truly relaxed and able to talk freely.

Knowing he would never be the big boss Joey had moved to the cottage full time. While he still reported to his older brother, Joey has become the unofficial boss for the Galena territory. People on vacation still needed drugs. They still wanted to place bets on games. Every so often, they wanted the company of a woman. His crew could provide services and funnel some extra income back to Anthony in the big city.

Greg laughed to himself at how Joey likely had the most profitable legitimate business run by the DeRege family. There were five different colleges within a half hour drive. Joey set up a small studio and professionally managed both girls and boys doing webcam modeling and OnlyFan pages. As a legitimate business, it was a cash cow, and an easy tool for laundering ill-gotten money.

His drive across highway twenty was faster than he assumed. Traffic had been light and kept moving at a reasonable pace. When the GPS announced a turn, Greg nearly missed it. He had been told the cottage was in a remote area but was not expecting an unmarked road off the highway. He had to turn onto two other narrow roads without street signs before pulling into a gravel driveway. A quarter mile down the driveway, Greg finally saw the cottage he was stopping at.

The house was enormous. Stone with timber framing made it look like a hunting lodge found out west. Set in a heavily wooded area the building almost vanished into the scenery. Greg guessed it had to be about five thousand square feet. He understood why the younger brother would want to live here versus some condo in the city.

A man dressed in khaki pants and a blue flannel shirt stood at the main door. As Greg opened his car door the man called out, "Are you Officer Messina?"

"Yeah, why?"

"Joey's ain't too keen on uninvited house guests. He also don't like guns dat ain't in da' possession of one of his guys. So leave da' sidearm in da' car."

"Anthony sent me here to meet with Joey."

"Dis is Joey's house. Don't care his brother sent you. Don't care you're a cop. You don't work for Joey, so dat" He pointed at the gun holstered on Greg's hip "will stay out here."

Pulling the holster off his belt, Greg said, "Fine. Christ, I got better things to do than stand out here and argue."

Chapter Eight

S tunned by Bob's revelation, Stu took a few seconds before saying. "Are you sure you want to make a comment like that?"

"Is true."

"Bob, I think maybe we should ask Detective Herrisch in here before you say much more."

Shaking his head in the negative. "No. You always good to me. I talk to you. I don't know this Herrisch detective person. No want to talk to him."

"Actually, Detective Herrisch is a she."

"Please give her my apologies for assuming she is a man."

"I will," Stu Said. "There is a protocol for talking to someone confessing to a crime."

"Argh... I watch police shows. Already know my rights. No lawyer can help me. Is best deal for me to be honest and ask you for help before *they* come for me."

Stu could not help but to think Bob was slipping back into his routine crazy talk. By mentioning someone coming for him. Many disturbed people talked about conspiracy theories where shadow groups were after them. However, the average citizen in small town America was so unimportant it was unlikely they were being hunted by some anonymous group.

"Okay, Bob, do you mind if I step out and talk to my boss? I don't want to screw anything up by talking to you. Last thing I need is to get in trouble for talking to you."

"Yes, yes, is okay. No need to lose job over little old me."

Too many people were milling around the hallway of the hospital. Stu wanted some privacy for this phone call. The staff break room might offer him solitude, but Stu did not dare go there. He sat in that break room too many times with Christina. When both were working nights, they would coordinate to take a meal break together.

Time heals all wounds. Life was feeling close to normal without her. Putting himself in places to stir up memories tore open some wounds. Stu could not avoid the Emergency Room all the time. Being an officer, it was part of his job to bring folks under arrest for medical clearance. He could however avoid the backrooms of the hospital where personal precious moments had taken place.

Looking around, Stu tried to decide where to go. Out to the parking lot to his car seemed almost too far. What if the Chief asked a question and Stu needed to check for an answer? It would be embarrassing to have the Chief waiting on him to walk all the way back inside. The stairwell seemed to be the best option. Most people seemed to use the elevators. The few that did not ride the elevator used fancy open stairs at the lobby. At the end of the hall was the emergency stairs.

Scrolling down his contacts, Thompson pulled up Chief Ruiz's listing. The Chief did not mind calls at home. While the man rarely came to work in a uniform to actively participate, the Chief did like to keep involved with how cases were progressing.

"This is Ruiz."

"Hi Chief. It's Stu calling. Need to talk about something quick."

"Son, you better not be calling to quit on me."

"Don't worry," Stu Said. "No planning to quit anytime soon. Which is why I was calling. Don't want to do something that would get me fired." Stu could hear a chuckle from the other end of the phone.

"All right. Tell me what it is you needed to talk about."

"Well sir, Bob, the crazy guy who walks around town, just woke up. He asked to talk to me."

"Why would he want to talk to you?"

Stu explained Bob had asked for one of a short list of officers. "Because I was at the PD, Sgt. Noris sent me over versus calling someone else in."

"Interesting. Go on."

"It seems Bob is not as crazy as we think. Turns out English is his second language. People assumed he was crazy and so he never worked to change our opinion."

Police Chief Ruiz asked Stu what this had to do with needing their phone call.

"Bob asked me about fingerprints. Sounds like he overheard the reserve deputy talking to a nurse. He then admitted to being a hitman."

"Wait. He said what?"

"He made a spontaneous utterance informing me he had killed people."

"What did you do?"

"Excused myself from the room and called you."

"Young man, you need to explain this to me in detail again."

Stu took a few minutes to explain everything Bob had said. The Chief kept quiet listening, only adding short "uh-huh" and "okay" statements to show he was still on the phone. During his explanation, Stu pointed out Bob indicated *'they'* might come for him.

"Who does he think they are?"

"Don't know, sir. Did not want to ask. Miranda issues and not wanting to mess up the case. That is why I am calling. Do you want me to keep talking to him, or should I walk away?"

"Good question." Chief Ruiz was silent for a beat. "You have a rapport with him. He asked to talk to you specifically. I would say that if he wants to keep talking, then yes, you stay there and listen to him. But make sure you read Miranda and record the conversation.

"Sounds good chief. What about the cop coming up from St. Louis? Do I need to worry about talking to Bob before he gets here?"

"The way I see it, he wants to tell his story. All you are going to do is listen. Don't interrogate him, asking loads of questions. Let him do the talking and if the folks from St. Louis get upset that will be their problem."

After saying their goodbyes, Stu hung up and ran down the steps to his car. The only way he had to record their conversation was with his cell phone. With its battery already down to sixty percent, Stu wanted to grab the charging cable to ensure the phone would not die early on him.

"Okay, Bob, are you sure you want to talk to me?"

"Yes please. If I talk, you might get me deal before they come for me. Talking best option for me."

Stu explained he was going to need to record their conversation. He then plugged in his cell phone and set it on the rolling bed-side table. Tapping the screen, Stu activated an audio recorder app and started the recording. "This is officer Stuart Thompson of the Platteville Police badge number twenty-seven. I am at Southwest Medical Center with Libertino Bosso." Stu then read off the Miranda rights to Bob. "Do you wish to have a lawyer?"

"No."

"Are you willing to give a statement or answer questions?"

"Yes."

"First can you state your name and spell it for me?"

"Si... er, yes. Libertino Bosso." Bob then slowly spelled out his name. Once complete he said, "but everyone called me Bob, so feel free to call me Bob, spelled B as in bravo, O as in ocean, B as in bravo."

Stu bit his lip to keep from laughing that Bob had spelled out his nickname phonetically as well. "Thank you Libertino —"

"Please call me Bob. No one uses Libertino anymore and the people who do, I do no care much for. Now you want me to tell you about people I kill. Right? So, should I tell you that or you have other questions first?"

"You asked to talk to me, so I will let you decide what you want to talk about."

"I am the personal hitman for Anthony DeRege of the Chicago DeRege family. During my employment with him, I have killed twenty-two people on his orders. Early in my career I was kind of naïve. It is likely that I left some fingerprints behind on the scene. Mr. DeRege warned me he thought the police had a lead on me. I almost thought he was going to kill me, instead he had some men teach me about cleaning up scenes. One of them recommended I watch shows like *CSI*, which I do."

Stu suddenly knew who the *'they'* were that Bob was talking about. A person like Bob had some deep inside information about crimes committed by or in the name of a major crime boss. Actually, Bob had just admitted to firsthand knowledge of murders tied right to the head of the DeRege family.

A chill ran down Stu's spine. Could the mafia find out Bob was in an accident? More likely how long will it take for them to find out their hitman had been hurt? What happens when the DeRege family finds out Bob is in the hospital? Will someone come to kill Bob or maybe try to aid him in an escape?

"When you say that they are going to come for you, you are meaning DeRege's people, right?"

"Si... Yes... The boss will want to make sure I am not talking to the police. He will send a capodecina to check on me."

"Hold on" Stu said. "A capodecina?"

"Ah... how you say here... a Capo. It means leader of ten. They run the actual crews and report to the under bosses who then report to the big boss."

His only knowledge of the mob coming from watching The Sopranos and various movies, Stu felt pained trying to wrap his head around a Capo coming to town. He was also trying to figure out why a hitman would live in little old Platteville versus Chicago. "Wait, how would they know you are in the hospital? It's not like your name was in the paper as being hurt. We just figured it out for Christ's sake."

"We make the message normal days. If I don't message, he want to know why."

"Does he call you? You did not have a cell phone on you when you got hurt. With your permission, I could go get your phone."

"No... sorry no cell phone. Never got one. No like the idea that people could track me. Boss says FBI can listen in too easy also."

"Oh, yeah right. So landline phone. We could have the phone company forward your calls here."

Bob shook his head. "The FBI was listening in on landline phones long before the cell phones became so popular."

Sometimes people just don't offer information. As one academy instructor always said, if you don't ask the question people are not going to give you the answer. "Okay, so, do you guys meet in person some place?"

"No, too risky if same people keep meeting at regular, or even semi-regular intervals. FBI has people tailing members of the DeRege family. They see me with them, they know I am connected to the family. Whole reason for me to be in this town is to keep me, how you say, under grid."

What Bob was saying could easily be mistaken for the ranting of a crazy man. Police often encounter citizens claiming the FBI, CIA or some other three letter agencies are tracking them. Problem was most of these people are so averagely average there would be no reason to track them. If not for the fingerprints found murder scenes Stu would have assumed Bob was one of the crazies. Before talking to him, Stu had assumed Bob was mentally disturbed.

"I think you mean under the radar."

"Ah... si, yes, keep under the radar is what I was told to do."

"So, how do you communicate with this guy?"

"Easy. We use chalk marks on the sidewalk. Anthony DeRege's cousin came up with the idea. Guy reads all kinds of spy novels. We have multiple locations in the city. His men make a mark. The location is dependent on the day and if the date is even or odd. I have locations to then also leave a mark.

We each have different symbols, circles and arrows to note simple messages. They check to see if I okay, if I need more money than my allowance and to tell me they have job for me to do. I have marks saying I am fine, asking for money and that I have received the information on who to kill."

Chapter Nine

"Greg, come sit. Long time no see." Joey DeRege was a true little brother to Anthony. He was shorter in stature, only about five and a half feet tall. Also, he was slim, less than one hundred and sixty pounds.

"Yeah, it has been a while." Greg sat on the end of a plush leather sofa. The great room of this house was larger than his apartment back in Chicago. Wood walls with a two story rock faced fireplace flanked by floor to ceiling windows gave the room an extra grand appearance. Looking around, Greg thought how Joey was more suited to the rural life than in the big city. The smaller man never fit in with Anthony's crew back in Chicago.

"We have a bit of a problem."

"That is what your brother told me when he ordered me here." Greg resented the fact the DeRege family had blackmailed him into being a crooked cop. They always acted all friendly, but there was also the undertone of an unsaid threat.

Joey must not have picked up on Greg's sarcasm in using the word "ordered." Or if he picked up on it Joey ignored it as he kept his tone friendly. "We have a man who lives up the road from here in Wisconsin. Someone who is like family to us but who is not an official member of the family. He belongs to the fingerprint you talked to my brother about."

"Who is he?"

"His name is Libertino."

Greg realized Joey would not tell him anything unless he asked the questions. Typical tough guy talking, only answers a question directly, nothing extra. "Okay, so who the hell is this Libertino to you guys and why were his fingerprints at some crime scenes?"

Pausing, Joey seemed to ponder how to answer the question. "He is someone my brother found on a vacation back to Italy. Anthony saw skill and promise in him, so my brother brought him over here. Which was great for me because Libertino solidified the idea of me living out here full time."

"Okay, so why do you need me here?"

"We need to know why the police ran his fingerprint. Do they have him in jail? If the police have him in custody, what it is for? What has he told the police about us? Most importantly, we might need you to shut him up."

"Woah... hold on a second. I might have to shut him up?"

"Yes. His whole reason for being over in Wisconsin was to keep him separate from the family. An outsider with no links. He still has knowledge about us. So if they have compromised him we can't let him disappear into witness protection."

"You are going to need to give me more information about this guy."

Joey looked taken aback. He was not used to people challenging him. The little brother of the big boss typically gave an order and people follow it. Even as a crooked cop, Greg did not feel he was fully beholden to Joey. "Like what?"

"Tell me who this guy is. Like what the hell he does for you? You know, maybe tell me how his fingerprints were at two murder scenes."

"I thought that much was obvious. But if I have to spell it out for you *officer,* I will. Libertino's prints are at the murder scenes because he killed the fuckers."

Greg felt like he was connecting the dots. All the facts had been disjointed. The investigator in him could not figure out the missing link. Greg had been assuming the fingerprints pointed to a killer, but the small town Wisconsin angle never fit. "Wait, are you telling me Anthony has been keeping a hitman living off the grid?"

"Yes."

"I don't mean to speak out of turn, but keeping this guy over here and having you out this way. Could that link the hit man to you? Are you the fall guy to protect your brother if people find out who the killer is?"

"No, not exactly."

"You got to stop playing coy with me. If I have to deal with the local cop and fix this problem, I need to know as much about the situation as possible."

"Have you ever met my cousin Bennet? He is a lawyer."

"No, can't say I have met him."

"Bennet grew up reading all kinds of spy novels. He saw a James Bond movie and next thing you know he is reading all kinds of tales about spies and assassins. Anyhow, one day he was telling my brother an idea to keep parts of the family safe in the age of the NSA, reading emails and text messages.

"His idea was to have someone, a hitman, with zero contact with the family. We created a system of leaving chalk marks at specific spots on specific days of the week. Marks had meaning like we have a job for you, or no jobs keep waiting, payment waiting, items waiting at location X or location Y. For the other guy he had marks as well. Such as: message received, need money early, mission complete. Then we also got a few spots for dead drops."

"A dead drop?" Greg knew what the term was. He was just surprised to hear it coming out of Joey's mouth.

"Yeah, got a few spots in some alleys and side streets with loose bricks. Also, out in some parks, the bathrooms at the pavilions have a little ledge up under the sink that can hold a larger envelope without anyone seeing it."

Greg was impressed. Using this old school trade craft would make it hard for investigators to track people involved. It also would hinder aspects of a normal modern investigation, such as wiretaps and warrants for emails. The random aspect of it would make it a nightmare for any officer trying to establish a pattern of operation.

"Alright, so I get this Libertino is the hitter. But who the fuck is he and why would he agree to this lifestyle?"

"Like I said, Anthony met him on a trip to Italy. Young man full of piss and vinegar. I was not there, but apparently he killed a guy right in front of my brother. Anthony brought him over here to escape, but at the cost of being an indentured servant."

"So how the fuck did he end up in Platteville?"

"My brother is a die hard Bears fan. Back in the eighties till the early two thousands the Bears did a summer training camp out of town.

Get the rookies away from the temptations of the big city. The college at Platteville hosted them every July and August. I always thought we should expand our family's reach out to Galena. So Anthony put me in charge of operations over here, including running out an anonymous hitman."

"But why here? Why not keep him here under wraps in the city?"

"If he lived back home, he would know about our daily operations. We needed the separation of the dead drops. My cousin, the lawyer, was insistent on how to run the perfect murder operation. We don't operate in Wisconsin, that is the Gallo family, out of Milwaukee territory. So, us planting someone up there adds one more layer of removal from our family's operation."

Greg contemplated what he had been told. "So I need to do a little reconnaissance to find out why the local cops are running his prints. Then what?"

"Make sure he does not talk."

"I get that. But how should I do it? Contact Anthony to get a lawyer up here ASAP?"

"No, you kill him."

"I can't just kill some guy. Especially if he is in police custody."

Joey's voice took on an agitated edge. "Why not? You cops do it all the time. Claim he attacked you and went for your gun. Fuck, we can make it easier. I got some untraceable guns. I will give you one. Shoot the gun and plant the gun on him. People will believe the small-town police missed a little .380."

As a rookie officer, Greg had been in a shooting. He and two other officers were confronting two men matching the description of robbery suspects. One man pulled a gun and shot the officer next to Greg in the vest. The officer was hurt, but the vest saved his life. All three cops returned fire, killing the suspect. The medical examiner ruled the fatal shot was from the officer hit in the vest. His round went into the suspect's neck and up into the head. Greg's shot had gone into the suspect's stomach.

In his mind, Greg always minimized his actions at the shooting. Yes, he had shot someone, but it would only have wounded the suspect. His partner actually killed that suspect.

The shooting had also helped him make detective faster than most of his peers. The stress of that shooting pushed him to hang out with the group of guys who frequented bars and clubs. Which had led him down the path of sleeping with Summer, which was videotaped by the DeRege family. A split second of time snowballing to where he was now.

Where was he now?

He was being asked to kill a man. Not in self defense, but to execute someone he never met. Shooting that suspect was true self defense. That suspect had shot first. It was a trained response for Greg to shoot back. There was no thought, no malice, just a reaction to the event. Now he was being asked, no he was being told, to murder a man.

He did not know if he could do it. However, he needed to put on a good front. Make it look as if he was committed to the mission. "Sounds good. Get me a drop gun and I will get this wrapped up as quick as I can."

"Good to hear." Joey told Greg to wait as he stood and left the room. Five minutes later the mob underboss returned with a small nylon gun case. Setting it on the coffee table, Joey motioned for Greg to open it.

Inside was a North American Arms Guardian. A silver compact semi-automatic handgun just under five inches long that could hide in a pants pocket. Greg was familiar with the company. They were known for making small, easy to conceal guns. Also, in the case, was a loaded magazine and two thousand dollars in cash.

"My brother said to give you a little walking around money to cover any expenses in completing this task. You should know that when you come back, we will have ten times that amount waiting for you as a thank you."

Twenty thousand dollars. Was that what a human life was worth? Then again, Greg had investigated scenes of business owners killed by robbers over only a few hundred bucks from a cash register. Just a reminder that a person's life was worthless to others.

"This gun have a history I need to worry about?"

"Nah... remember a few years back the guys who got convicted of buying guns in Madison and then driving down to Chicago to sell them to gang bangers?"

"Yeah, couple of school teachers, right? They got so many guns the store owner gave them a discount. They mostly sold to felons who could not legally buy in a gun shop. Claimed at the time of arrest, they sold at gun shows to collectors."

"Those are the guys. Gang members were happy to pay twice retail to them for guns. All the guns gangbangers sell to each other are cheap crap. Poorly maintained, broken, many already used in prior crimes. Those teachers were selling new fully working guns. Clean of any involvement in past crimes. They made a mint. Had a reputation for a quality product that gangbangers would pay out the ass for. We got some guns off them as well. So this one is clean. Paper trail leads back to the teachers, who happen to already be in prison for illegal gun sales."

Looking at the box, Greg thinks for a moment. "Yeah, a shooting might bring too much attention to this situation. Any chance you got some pure heroin and a needle? I have an idea, but will keep this gun as a backup plan."

Chapter Ten

Bob had given Stu a fairly solid outline of how he operated for the DeRege family. The one thing Stu still had not found out was how he actually ended up living in Platteville.

"Okay Bob, can you explain to me how it is you ended up here in Platteville?"

"I tell you already. Anthony DeRege move me here to hid out and do jobs when needed."

"Yeah, I got that. But how? Like when did you meet him? Why here in Platteville versus just keeping you under warps down in Chicago?"

"Ah... yes, you want the more facts."

Stu nodded his head. "That would help me understand this all better."

"My family owned a restaurant in the village of Capaci, in the Province of Palermo. It is a beautiful little city right on the sea at the north end of the island of Sicily. You might have heard of it. The Sicilian families blew up a judge with a bomb hidden in a culvert under the roadway driving down the highway through town."

Stu shook his head. "Sorry, not a case I have heard of. Then again, organized crime has never been an interest of mine. Arsonist and history of fire is more my passion."

"You should look up the case. Very interesting. Bombs are like fire, so you might find some information that you like."

"I will have to look it up." Stu was sincere. The bombing had piqued his curiosity. "Anyhow, you were saying about your father owning a restaurant?"

"Ah, yes. We had a location close to the beach. Good tourist traffic you know. Because of our location we had to pay the tax to the local family."

"You mean protection money?"

"More like extortion monies. When you pay the criminals to keep you safe from criminals, how is that protection? I asked my dad that many times. He always tell me same thing. Shut up and keep the head down."

Stu wished he had more knowledge of how crime families worked. The way the conversation was going he felt it might become a crash course. "How much did he pay?"

"It always depended on who was collecting. Mostly it was midlevel crew members came around once a week to collect. Often times it was they got a meal for free and then took a few hundred dollars from the till. Very business like... how you say... down the low key.

"Every so often a junior street level man might come in. When they came, it was like a robbery, more than a protection payment. These guys would not care if we had just paid. They say it was a special week and so we needed to pay extra special payment. They go behind the bar, open the register and take nearly all the money. Often times they took alcohol from the bar as well. I always assumed the low level guys had not been authorized by the family. Street hustlers trying to get a few extra bucks to get high under the guise of official family business."

"When did Anthony DeRege come into the picture?"

"He came in with three other guys and one of the local middle level crew members. My father was told that DeRege was an out-of-town guest. He was to get a free meal and drinks. My father paid the tax for the week and the midlevel guy left. The DeRege's ate well and continued to drink for a short time. It was not extravagant, so my father was in a good mood. Happy to oblige the out-of-town guests. He figured the local family would show some appreciation for our hospitality. Then right about the time we would normally close Enzo came in."

"Who is Enzo?"

"Enzo was one of the low level thugs that would come in to extort extra protection from my dad. He was the worst of them. It was not unusual for him to hit my father or mother. He always emptied the register. My father would beg him to allow us to keep some money to pay bills. Enzo's answer was always the same, a punch and a threat of killing us."

"So you got some Chicago Mafia bigwigs in the restaurant and this thug comes in. Something go sideways?"

"Si... Yes... I don't think Enzo knows we have guests, and we had just paid our weekly tribute. He walked up to my dad with his wild look. To this day I swear he was high. Tells my dad to empty the register. My dad looked to the table DeRege was at. Enzo hits my dad and yells at my dad if he does not pay he will deal with the Capo. I saw one of DeRege's guys starting to stand. Like he was going to help. But when Enzo said Capo, Anthony motioned for the man to sit.

"I was in the kitchen watching from the door frame. My father says he just paid a few hours ago and Enzo hits him again. Knocks him down to the floor. Then Enzo pulled out a knife. Says my father has five seconds to get up and empty the register or he will kill my father."

Stu was on the edge of his seat. He never imagined working in an average Wisconsin city would he ever be listening first hand to a mafia killer telling his personal history.

"My father got up and walked behind the bar. Once the till was open, he turned and asked if Enzo had a bag to carry the money. Enzo got so mad. He reached over the bar, grabbed my father by his hair and slammed his face into the bar. When my father came up, there was blood everywhere. His nose had to be broken, it sat on his face wrong. Before my father could move, Enzo slammed his face down again, then held my father down. Enzo put his knife to my father's ear and said he was going to cut his ear off."

Bob's voice had trailed off. He was looking off into space now. Deep in thought, like his words had triggered a memory that was playing out as a waking dream. Stu gave Bob a minute to think. "What happened next?"

"Sorry?"

"You said this Enzo guy was holding your dad's head down on the bar and was about to cut his ear off."

"Oh... si... si... mi dispiace, I'm sorry. I was standing in the kitchen door. Watching Enzo hold my father down like that I was afraid he was going to kill him. I had to do something. So I walked up behind Enzo. I did not realize I had a knife in my hand till the blood started spraying out.

"In the movies they do a good job of showing blood, but it is not exactly right, you know? It does not gush out more of a squirting. And it is warm. I recall being surprised how warm the blood was."

It took an effort for Stu to keep seated. "Where did you stab him?"

"No, not stab. I slit his neck."

A chill ran down Stu's spine. He knew the man was a killer but was not expecting to hear such a matter-of-fact description of a murder. Maybe a case could have been made for self defense. Still, Bob's voice had been so free of any emotion. "Then what happened?"

"He died. I remember he slouched down and then rolled to look at me. He had this look like... like he could not believe it was me who had killed him. I had a reputation for being a, how you say... wall flower. Very shy, always worked in back in kitchen never out front with customers."

Thinking about some rumors over the years about Bob, Stu had to laugh. People had been way off the mark. This guy was not crazy, he was some kind of sociopath.

"At that time, Anthony was not the boss yet. His father was. I think he was twenty-two, maybe twenty-three. I know I had just turned nineteen. It was interesting he was looking at me. Not with fear, not with pity, but with something more like an admiration.

"My father started to cry. He was very scared. Did not know what was going to be worse, the police or the people Enzo worked for. Anthony stood up and motioned to his men. Without a word they took Enzo's body to our kitchen. One of them came out and started to clean Enzo's blood by the bar. Anthony was talking to my father. I do not speak English at that time so I don't know what they said.

"The two in the kitchen soon came out. My father told me to go back to kitchen and open back door. I saw four garbage bags sitting by the back door. One of Anthony's men pulled a car into the alley behind our building. The man pointed at the bags, then opened the trunk of car. So I put the bags in the car."

Stu felt stupid for asking as soon as the words came out. "Was Enzo in the bags?"

"I think so, yes. I did not see him in the kitchen, so bags only place his body could have gone."

"What about all the blood?"

"We did some of our own butchering at the restaurant. So blood was no big deal. Hose it all down the floor drain."

Given what Bob had been saying Stu questioned if he should call the FBI on this. He had an officer coming up from St. Louis in connection to open murders there. However, this case quickly was growing to encompass more than just a simple homicide.

Granted in the last few years, the FBI seems less interested in cases such as this. If Bob did not have written orders from Anthony DeRege, the case was based only on hearsay evidence. Lawyers would rip Bob apart. Without fingerprints, or DNA linking DeRege to the deaths in St Louis the case would be weak.

About the only option would be for Bob to have on a wire and record Anthony talking about the crimes. Unlikely, that would happen based on the cloak and dagger system Bob had mentioned before. "So you kill this guy and your dad fears reprisal from the local mob. How did that land you here in Platteville?"

"After I load bags in car, guys come thru kitchen tell me to get in car. My Father was there says to me to go with men and I be safe. That was the last time I see my home.

"We went to a hotel in Palermo. One guy takes my photo bunch of times. Two days later package comes with an American driver license and passport. Has my photo, but not my name. Had name of Wayne

Johns. Anthony says it now my new name, stupid name I vow to never use unless absolutely needed. We go to the airport and get on plane to US.

"When we get to US, Anthony introduces me to his baby brother Joey. Joey takes me on a plane ride to Dubuque. Then we drive to this cottage in the woods. Joey explained to me what my new job was. Well, he had a guy who translated for me. Teach me chalk marks and places to look for them or make them.

"After a week at the cottage Joey has guy give me ride here. Guy gives me keys to apartment over Jewelry store on Main Street. Says mine to live in. Next day I go for walk looking for chalk mark. When I see it I make one in return. Been that way for twenty-six years now."

"And the only task you ever did for them was kill people?"

"Si... yes, mostly folks trying to stick their noses into the DeRege family business. A good number of motorcycle gang members, a few Mexican cartel types and couple of time I hit made men from other families."

"Local cops found a knife at two scenes in St. Louis. Had your prints on it. You always use a knife?

"Mostly. But some people you can't always get that close to so sometimes I shot people. I think they liked it when I used a knife. Not sure why I did it the first time, but I just left the knife in the guy. Got a note from Joey saying how leaving the knife in the dead guy's chest was a great touch. So it became my... how do you say it... phoning card?"

"I think you mean your calling card."

Chapter Eleven

The drive from DeRege's cabin to Platteville was mostly a straight line on one highway. Just across the state line into Wisconsin Greg stopped for gas in a village called Hazel Green. While stopped, Greg figured he should hit the bathroom and get a coffee.

Stepping out of the bathroom, Greg found himself face to face with a shorter, overweight man in a police uniform. "Hey there, Officer Schroder with the Hazel Green police. Mind if he had a quick little chat?"

"Sure is there a problem?"

"Hope not. See we got a nine one one call from a lady who said she noticed a gun on your hip when you were cleaning your windows."

"I thought CCW was legal in Wisconsin?"

The uniform cop moved his right hand to rest on his belt next to his duty firearm. "We do, but she was concerned because you got Illinois plates. Fairly sure with all the anti-gun feelings out of Illinois they don't issue many conceal carry weapon permits."

"Ah, I bet that is a common misconception outside the state. Chicago has a ton of anti-gun laws. But the rest of the state lives in a world of reality." Holding his hand mid chest level with the palms open as a sign of non-combativeness. "As a matter of fact, I am Chicago PD. Just taking a brief road trip up to Platteville for a few days."

"Interesting, will need to see some ID."

"Sure officer. It is in my wallet in my back right pocket. How would you like me to retrieve it?"

Officer Schroder paused for a second. Greg assumed he had never dealt with a situation like this before. Likely had trained once in the academy for it, but never reinforced that training by needing to do it. "Ah, just use your left hand to reach back for it." It was not the worst way to handle the situation, but Greg would have done it differently.

"Sure, I am going to keep my right hand visible here as I reach for my wallet with my left." Slowly, Greg got his wallet out and held it up for the officer to see. Flipping it open, he revealed his Chicago PD badge and Police identification card. Fake badges were easy to get on the internet. An ID card with the department logo and photo of the officer in uniform was something most folks failed to get with a fake badge. Greg held the wallet out for the officer to take.

After a few seconds of inspection, Officer Schroder hands it back. His body language shifted from a formal tense posture to a more relaxed, conversational stance. "I hate digging around in people's wallets. Mind pulling out your driver's license. I need to call it in to dispatch just for the CAD record." Computer aided dispatch, or CAD, an in-house database system recording basic info about police actions. Greg knew it was routine, so he handed over his license without complaint. Better to seem friendly and give this cop less reason to ask too many questions.

Using the radio mic on his shoulder, the officer called the information into his dispatcher. "So what has you heading up to Platteville?"

A good lie was built on bits of truth. "An officer there entered the prints of a suspect into the system that are linked to some crimes I have an interest in. Want to see if they can get me in touch with this suspect. Maybe I can close out some open files back home."

"Cool. You know what officer ran the prints?"

"A Detective Thompson I think it was."

Schroder chuckles. "Thompson is not actually a detective. Just a patrol officer, but he is a CSI guru. Super nice guy. But, I have to warn you his girlfriend was murdered a few months back. So if he seems cold give him some slack... okay."

"Thanks for that info. I will watch what I say so as to not talk about family stuff around him. I think it was a lucky thing that lady call you on me."

Before he could respond, Officer Schroder's radio announced that Greg Massana had a valid Illinois Driver License. "Well cool. Glad I could help. Sorry for the inconvenience of stopping you like this."

Walking towards the coffee machines in the gas station, the two cops made some chit chat. Mostly shop talk about working conditions and management expectations. Walking towards the counter to pay, the clerk waved Greg off. "Story policy. Cops get one free coffee a day. I saw your badge before, so that one is on the house." Officer Schroder gave him a pudgy faced smile and nod.

Shrugging his shoulders, Greg thanked the lady for the coffee, said goodbye to the village cop, and pushed open the door.

Greg checked into his hotel room before stopping at the police department. Before leaving, he had made a reservation online with the Country 7 Hotel, a modestly priced chain hotel. Looking over Google maps at the time, he made the reservation Greg saw it was on one of the major roads in town. It was also a perfect distance to multiple fast-food restaurants and a pharmacy.

The clerk barely said anything during check in, she seemed to have little interest in him. Taking a glance over the counter, he saw a textbook and a notebook. Front desk at a hotel, as long as it was not busy, an easy way to make money while getting homework done. If things went sideways, it was better she not remember much about him.

His room was decent. Single king size bed facing a dresser with a flatscreen television. Couch off to the side with a coffee table and desk. A small refrigerator and microwave in a cabinet between the dresser and desk. Greg didn't need more, he was not here to hang out in the hotel room.

Checking the closet, he found a safe with instructions on how to program his own combination into the touchpad. Tossing the gun, heroin and half the cash Joey gave him into the safe, Greg closed it. He doubted he could act tonight. Better to keep those items locked away for now.

Next, he stopped at the pharmacy. It was a different chain than the one he used in Chicago, however this one was a vendor of the same brand of prepaid visa cards he used. He loaded five hundred dollars onto his card while keeping the other five hundred in cash in his wallet.

Finally, he pulled into a public parking lot a block away from the police station. Not having a squad car made him feel self-conscious. It was likely nothing, but his worry was an officer asking why he had his personal car when on official police business.

"How can I help you?" A voice came out of a box set in the wall next to the doors. It had surprised him to find the door locked when he pulled on them. Then he noticed a sign listing the weekdays hours the lobby was open. Under the sign sat a button labeled "press for help".

"I am here to see Officer Thompson" Greg held his badge up to the camera over the door.

BUUUUZZZZZ... the sound of the electric lock releasing came off the door.

"Come into the lobby and then come in the first door on your right."

Greg did as instructed. Inside the lobby, he saw a door straight ahead labeled "Community room". To the right was a counter with bullet-proof glass. No receptionist sat behind the glass. Next to that counter was the door he had been told to go to. Upon his approach, it also buzzed, signaling it unlocked.

On the other side of the door was a hallway. The right side of the hall was lined with doors. The left had a single door, then opened out into cubicles. A voice came from the door on the left. "In here."

Following the voice, Greg found himself in a dispatch center. There were work stations for three people to work the phones and radios, but only one person was sitting at a console. Male about twenty years old. He had shaggy hair and a few days' growth on his face. From where he stood, Greg could see the dispatcher had on a t-shirt from one of the popular police webpages. No doubt it had some embarrassing slogan on the back few real cops would appreciate wearing in public.

"I'm Carl. You must be the guy from St. Louis, Mike, right?"

"Huh?"

"You said you were here to see Stu... err... Officer Thompson. He said a guy from St. Louis might show up." Looking down at a note on the desk. "Detective Mike Radvich was the guy he talked to on the phone but Stu was expecting you on Monday. "

Suddenly, Greg felt his job might be a bit easier. If they assumed he was this Radvich guy he could do what needed to be done then take off without any links back to Chicago. Assuming this St. Louis cop did not show up early. "Yeah, bosses back home didn't think we should wait."

"Oh, I bet. Stu was up at the hospital talking with Bob but is coming back into the PD. Should I radio him to let him know you are here."

"Bob?"

"That is the nickname we gave the John Doe. Hey... you got a name for him?"

"Nope, sorry. Was hoping you folks would, half the reason I am here. We put him in the system as a John Doe warrant, looking to get a name."

"Ohh... yeah, should have thought about it that way." Carl looked down at his table top. Greg got the feeling this kid got talked down to a lot. Likely a college student studying to be a cop, working dispatch part time to make his resume stand out. Kid like that could be in over his head as a dispatcher, resulting in officers putting him down a lot.

"You look young for a dispatcher there Carl. Let me guess, going to the college here in Platteville for Criminal Justice."

The kids perked back up. "Yeah."

"Good for you." Time to butter this kid up. Make him feel good about himself and then make a request. "When I was in college I worked in the comm center just like you. Made getting a job at the PD a piece of cake. Interview questions were so easy from experience handling stressful calls."

"That's what I thought when I applied for this job."

"Dispatching is hard. Between the phone, the radio and everyone wanting your attention at the same time. If you can do this, you can rock it out on the street."

A smile crept across Carl's face. "Thanks."

"It's the truth." Greg knew he had baited the kid well. Now to use it to his advantage. "While we wait, can you print off everything you have on this Bob guy in your CAD system?"

"Sure. Just give me a second." A few clicks of the mouse and the printer hummed. After the last page came out of the printer Carl handed the stack over to Greg. "Anything else?"

Greg looked at the last entry. A car crash. Bob was listed as a victim. Interestingly, an accident had kicked off this chain of events. "How about copies of the reports and statements from this crash he was in?"

Carl stood up. Walking past Greg into the hall, Carl said. "That case file is likely still over in the transcriptionist's office. She was in this morning typing up the officer's dictation. Files don't go to the records room till after officers approve the typed out version of the dictation." He was in the other room less than a second when he came back holding up a file. "You want everything in here?"

"Yes, please."

Carl turned and went down the hall, turning into the cubicles. The sound of a photocopier echoed into the dispatch center. Carl appeared back at the door frame. "It should only take a minute or two. I need to keep close to the radio and phone while the copier does its thing."

"Thanks Carl. You are a big help. I hope you know that."

Chapter Twelve

Turning the corner into dispatch, Stu saw a man he didn't recognize. He was sitting at one of the dispatching counsels talking to Carl. The two were deep into a discussion about a historical figure from police history. No doubt it had to do with the homework Carl was working on.

Clearing his throat Stu said "I am done at the hospital for today. But it looks like I might have some more work to do. Can you radio the sergeant to call me here at the PD."

"Yes sir. Oh... by the way Stu this is Mike Radvich from St. Louis."

"Hi, sorry, on the phone you made it sound like it would be tomorrow before you got here."

The man stood and offered his hand for a shake. "Out of state travel needs approval from the captain, who never works weekends. When I talked to the LT after our call she decided to call the captain at home. He agreed so I hit the road right away."

"Your timing is perfect."

"Oh how so."

"Our guy gave me permission to search his apartment. Got the key from his clothing at the hospital. Before we go I just want to alert the supervisor on-duty about what I am doing."

"Sounds like my timing is good. Assuming you are inviting me to help you check out this guy's place."

Nodding, Stu said. "Yes it might make things a bit cleaner. Chain of custody for the evidence wise. We find anything you want for your case in St. Louis. Better to say you were here when we collect it."

"He give you permission to take stuff from the apartment?"

"Yep, and yes I even have it in writing on a consent form. However, I still think we should get a warrant. Tonight we can go look around, then tomorrow morning after the judge signs the warrant we can dig in deeper."

"Why not have a judge sign a warrant tonight? Please don't tell me you can only get warrants during regular business hours of the courthouse."

"Nope, we can get warrants anytime. Calling judges at home after hours is something we try to limit. This guy is in the hospital and will not be able to get out for a few days. We have a deputy guarding him. I should be able to get a deputy to guard his apartment. This is not an emergency. We have lots of time, no need to piss off the judge."

"Okay. So what do you want me to do."

"Just chill here till after I talk to the sergeant."

Sitting at his cubicle in the officer work area Stu had an odd thought. This Mike guy had not asked who the John Doe was. He must have known Stu was at the hospital interviewing the suspect all day. If Stu was in that guy's shoes the first question he would ask would be to find out who John Doe is.

His thoughts were interrupted when Carl's voice came over the building PA system. "Officer Thompson, call waiting on line one."

Grabbing the receiver Stu hit the button labeled line one. "This is Thompson."

"What you got?" Asked the familiar voice of Sgt. Noris.

"Hey Sergeant, you are not going to believe this." Stu gave his supervisor a brief overview of what he had been told. Libertino, AKA Bob, was a hitman. Living in Platteville was his way of hiding in plain sight. He did not get into details about the chalk marks and daily walks. That was information for later.

"Interesting. Just goes to show you never know about people. We all assumed he was crazy, turns out it was just an act to keep us off his scent."

Not so much an act as the fact that English was his second language. Stu felt it was better to just let the sergeant keep his assumption rather than go deeper into explanation. Right now Sgt. Noris just needed to understand the big picture. Specific details could be filled in later.

"One other thing sir."

"What is it Stu?"

"Well, I guess two things. First, that detective from St. Louis made it here today. Second, Bob gave me permission to take a look in his apartment."

"Not sure how I feel about you going into his place based only on voluntary consent. This sounds like it could be a major case. What was the feeling from the guy from St. Louis?"

"I agree with you Sergeant. It would be better to have a warrant before doing too much. Detective Radvich seemed surprised I got permission. He wanted to make sure he could come with me is all he seemed to care about."

"So does that mean you are calling a judge today or what?"

"With your permission I want to just use the consent as a way to go into the apartment and look around. Take some photos and see what we see. Tomorrow we can get the warrant and process it completely."

"Why even go in tonight if you are willing to wait till tomorrow?"

"I want to know the scope of the scene. Is he a hoarder? How about if he has piles of firearms or any amount of explosives in there. We might need a ton of resources and want to get them lined up early so we are ready when it is time to do a real search."

"Fine. Take that guy from St. Louis with you. Just make sure you stick to the plan. Photos only, don't go digging in deep."

Stu assured Sgt. Noris he would do as they agreed then hung up the phone. Stepping into the door frame for the dispatch center he motioned for the person he thought was Detective Radvich to follow him. Together they headed to the basement of the police department. As they walked Stu pointed out department landmarks, sort of an impromptu mini tour of their facility.

Downstairs Officer Thompson went into the evidence processing room to grab his camera bag. "Do you have a camera with you?"

"No, didn't think to bring one."

"Not a big deal. You can have copies of all our photos. What size gloves are you?"

"Large"

Grabbing a box of gloves from a cabinet Thompson dropped them into the camera bag.

The apartment was only a block from the police department. Both officers agreed to just walk over. Located above a jewelry store, they accessed the apartment from a wide alley behind the building. Three parking stalls in the alley had signs designating them reserved for employees of the store.

Of all his years working for the police department, Stu had never had reason to go into the apartments at this building. Many of the buildings on Main Street had apartments above them. The average height was three stories, but a few went as high as five. Each building was a maze of halls containing multiple small single bedroom or studio apartments. A few buildings had a single multi bedroom unit per level.

Knowing the jewelry store was a long narrow storefront, Stu was not surprised to find this was a one unit per level style building. Bob said he was in unit three, as in the apartment on the third floor. There was no apartment one, just two and three. These numbers just signaled second and third floors versus total number of units in the place.

Inside, the apartment was neat and only had the most basic of furniture. The main room had a kitchen and a living room separated by a counter. There was not enough room for a kitchen table, so the counter was both a cooking and eating area. A couch sat on the south wall under the windows facing out towards Main street. The north wall had a television sitting on top of what looked like a coffee table.

Two doors were set into the west wall. Each going to a bed room. One room had a bed in it. The other had a pad on the floor along with a pull up bar and dip bar bolted to the wall. Both bedrooms had a door leading into the single bathroom for the apartment.

"This is an odd layout for an apartment" the out of town cop said.

"Yes, and no. Looking at how small the bedrooms are, I bet this was once a single bedroom unit. Likely had a larger living room with a breakfast nook that could fit a table. About thirty years ago the campus increased enrollment, but couldn't build dorms fast enough. Landlords found interesting ways to remodel spaces to fit more people. What had once been a single bedroom unit is now a two bedroom."

Stu started to snap some photos. The two men took their time looking in and around everything. Nothing out in the open caught their eye.

Kitchen cupboards contained a handful of plates and bowls. Basically enough for a single guy to eat one meal a day and only need to do dishes every other day. It was well stocked with food. Mostly health food and pastas, with little in the way of chips or candy. One cabinet was stocked with a dozen bottles of wine. The refrigerator was filled with fresh fruits, fish, and lean meats.

Bob had talked about his family owning a restaurant. He had mentioned a few times about working in the kitchen. Double checking the cookware Stu notices it was higher end copper pots and pans. The knife set looked expensive and was a brand name Stu had never seen at places like War-Wart. A shelf was filled with actual individual spices, not the premixed varieties found in most bachelor pads.

More parts of Bob's story were coming into alignment. He had been told to keep a low profile and keep to himself. So he did as ordered. As a trained cook he set himself up with as best a kitchen he could given the resources provided by the landlord.

Twenty-six years Bob said he lived in this apartment. If he was nine-teen at the time he left Italy, that made him forty-five. Keeping a low profile. A home gym in the second bedroom devoted to bodyweight workouts. No weights to drop, no excess noise to disturb neighbors.

He must have worked out daily to keep as trim and in shape as Bob looked.

"Hey got something in here."

Stu snapped back from his thoughts. The other officer was in the main bedroom. "What did you find?"

"A wallet. Want to come take a photo before I open it up."

"Give me a second."

A drawer in the nightstand held a passport and wallet. Stu took a few photos. Then the out-of-town officer opened them up. "Oh, this must be a fake. Wow, talk about an unoriginal name, Wayne Johns. You think this guy is trying to be some kind of badass taking on a moniker that is an anagram of John Wayne?"

"Don't think so" Stu said as he took a photo of the driver license.

"Why not?"

"Well first I don't think switching up the first and last names of a person makes it an anagram. Second when I was talking to him he said the ID was provided to him by his employer. Bob went on to tell me he hated the name and only used the ID when he needed it."

"So you're telling me Anthony DeRege came up with that shitty alias."

Pausing, Stu thought about how Bob had worded it. "I don't know if Anthony came up with it or if it was the mope who made the card. Bob just said they took his photo and disappeared for a while. Came back with the ID card and passport later. My guess is Anthony asked for the ID to be made and said he wanted an American sounding name for the guy, an easier way to get him out of the country and into the US."

"Sure but this ID was issued two years ago. This can't be the one he got over in Italy."

"Bob travels by bus to his targets. Likely he rents hotel rooms also. He needs a current ID card. I would imagine they have updated his credentials every so often."

The other officer made a comment about how Bob should have requested a name change when his ID was upgraded. Thompson wondered when he mentioned the DeRege family. The two cops had yet to talk about what Bob said at his interview today.

Chapter Thirteen

opefully, I will not have to kill Officer Stu Thompson, Greg Thought, *he is a decent guy.*

Sitting at the edge of the bed, Greg flipped the channel on the television. Not much on. Same old reality television crap he avoided watching at home. Trying to find something to watch, he thought about his night out with Officer Thompson.

After Searching Bob's apartment, the two men had gone out for a beer. A pizza restaurant on Main street that also had an Irish pub attached to it. Stu had explained while the restaurant was popular with university students the pub was too far from the popular college bars for most kids to seriously drink at.

Maintaining his guise as Mike from St. Louis, Greg exchanged stories of working in the big city. The stories he told were all true. He just changed the details, so the events did not take place back in Chicago. While they talked, a few people approached Stu to say hi. Mostly local business people, all of whom got introduced to *Mike.* They all knew enough not to ask too many questions about what a cop from out of town was up to.

The officer seemed to know nearly everyone. He passed it off as being a member of the local volunteer fire department besides being a cop. Being personable, he explained, helped him to be a good officer. Then he joked about being too skinny to be a jerk, so he needed to use his brain and mouth more than his muscle on the job.

Just before they called it a night, a group of college-age men in Purple jackets walked past on their way out of the restaurant towards the street. Seeing Stu, the group stopped. They were members of some fraternity that Stu had been a member of back when he was a student. There was a pride in Stu's voice when he introduced *Mike* to these guys. Almost like he was trying to show the younger generation that people from their organization will do something in life.

Stewie was what the kids in purple all called Officer Thompson. Actually, they called him Officer Stewie. After they left, he explained it had been his nickname in college. It was an obvious nickname with the popularity of the cartoon Family Guy for college aged males when he was an undergrad.

What kind of cop allows college kids to call him by a silly nickname like that?

The way Officer Thompson told it, his fraternity background helped to solve a major case recently. A serial rapist had been hitting the local campus hard. Even killed a few girls. A tip came in from a fraternity. They talked to Stu, knowing he would respect the Greek organization and minimize their exposure to the case.

I wonder how a guy like him would fare in Chicago?

It didn't matter. Greg was thinking he had a solid plan to put an end to Libertino, or Bob or whatever name they wanted to call him. In the morning, he would head up to the hospital. Greg checked online.

Doors opened at the hospital at six in the morning. Various rehab services started early. As long as the doors were open, patients could accept visitors.

With a badge, he could likely get access after hours. Nurses would scrutinize his reason for coming in and would lead to questions Greg didn't want to have to answer. Leaving the hospital might not be easy also if Libertino coded too fast from the heroin Greg planned to administer. Better to wait till normal business hours. Fewer questions, and fewer eyes on his every move.

When he left Stu, the plan was to meet at the Platteville Police station about nine in the morning. Stu had claimed visiting hours at the hospital did not start till nine in the morning. Why had Thompson lied? Greg felt the guy had been very upstanding till caught in this lie.

Get in. Inject the IV with heroin and get out. Once the mission was done, hit the road back to Galena to let Joey know the job was finished. Collect his cash and then get home to Chicago.

Frustrated with the lack of a good show, Greg turned off the television. Reaching across the nightstand for the lamp, he double checked the alarm. Laying back on the pillow mentally, he went back over his plans for the next day. Aided by a few beers, sleep came quickly for Greg.

His dreams had been about the bartender, Summer, and how she had duped him. It was almost like a nightmare. Replaying the events as he had lived them, Greg was cursing himself to stop. They were sitting on the couch in her apartment, kissing. In his dream, Greg was a ghost watching this going on from outside his own body.

It was like watching a movie of someone kissing Summer, except that someone looked just like Greg. When the dream image of Greg reached out for her breasts, he tried to reach out and swat Greg's hands away. But in the dream he was only an observer not able to interact with her or his doppelgänger.

Trying to yell, his voice was just a whisper. Turning around, he tried to walk out of her door. Only the exit in the dream flipped him right back into the same room. Nothing he did could stop his dream self from making the mistakes the real Greg has made.

Her top came off. Soon after, his pants were at his ankles. Summer's head was in the dream Greg's lap. The ghost of Greg closed his eyes, but his eyelids were see through. Holding his hand over this face, it to was clear. Ghost Greg was helpless to stop watching dream Greg having sex with the girl the mob paid to seduce him.

Ding, Da, Da, Ding Ding, Dong. Ding Da, Da, Ding Ding, Dong.

Snapped from the nightmare, Greg sat up. Looking around, it took him a moment to realize he was in a hotel room. The alarm on his cell phone was still singing its melody. Snatching up the phone, he silenced the alarm. Greg sat for a moment longer, resisting the urge to lay back down for a snooze.

Standing, he stumbled to the mini refrigerator for a Mountain Dew. Greg had not gotten drunk the night before drinking with Officer Thompson. He was. however, feeling dehydrated. The nightmare also had not provided him with restful sleep. Grogginess kept his mind in a haze, affecting his steps across the room.

Sitting at the foot of the bed, he took a long gulp of green caffeinated liquid. Closing his eyes, he could feel the stimulant effect of the soda leach out from his stomach towards his limbs. A second drink and the cobwebs in his brain dispersed.

Three more long pulls from the bottle and he felt ready to stand back up. This time, Greg was actually steady on his feet. Moving to the bathroom he started his morning routine.

With the car still running, Greg sat in the parking lot of the Platteville Community Hospital. Eyes closed, he listened to *The Reaper* by Blue Oyster Cult. Classic rock radio stations seemed to be the default for Greg. This song was prophetic, and he sat listening to calm his nerves.

40,000 men and women every day... Like Romeo and Juliet... 40,000 men and women every day...

It was correct that people die by the tens of thousands every day. Nobody knows when they are going to die. Heck, for all Greg knew this could be the day he dies. Once he completed this task, he could go see Joey DeRege, only to be shot to keep this Libertino that much more secret.

Don't fear the reaper

We'll be able to fly... don't fear the reaper

Baby, I'm your man...

The song was about the futility of fearing death. Don't fear the reaper, as in the grim reaper, taker of souls to the afterlife. Today Greg would be the reaper. He would take the life of Libertino. A man who had also taken many lives.

Taking a deep breath, Greg let it out slowly. His heart felt like it was about to break out from his rib cage. He felt a slight twitch in the muscles of his legs. That twitch was a feeling he had felt many times before. It was his body's natural reaction to an expected physical confrontation. The fight-or-flight reflex. Adrenaline being pushed to the muscles in an automatic response to fear.

Don't fear the reaper.

Why was Greg feeling fear? He was the reaper today. He had no reason to fear himself. Was it because he feared Libertino? The guy was in a hospital bed. There was nothing to fear.

Placing a hand in his pocket, Greg felt the needle already filled with heroin. Joey had given him pure, uncut product. Or as uncut as the DeRege family got it from their supplier. He had just over two hundred milligrams loaded into the syringe. At this purity level, for a person with no tolerance for regular drug use, the dosage was assured to be fatal.

Stepping from the car, Greg took a breath and hoped the fresh air would calm his nerves. It was a few minutes after seven in the morning. Hopefully, none of the hospital staff would think this was too early of an hour for the police to talk to the patient.

Greg already knew from the reports run off by the kid in dispatch what room Libertino was staying in. Getting off the elevator, Greg looked at the directory hanging on the wall to figure out which way towards the room. Last room on the left end of the hall. Turning, he noticed right away a young person standing in the hall wearing a sheriff's brown uniform.

Walking at a normal pace, Greg pointed, yet halfway covered the badge clipped to his belt. "Morning deputy. Is our suspect awake for me to talk to?"

"Excuse me?"

"Sorry, I'm Detective Mike Radvich. The guy in this room is a suspect in some murders in my jurisdiction. Came here last night to question him." Greg stood with his right hand resting on his belt right over his badge.

"Oh... sorry. You must be the guy from St. Louis. Yeah, Bob is an early riser. Been up a few hours now, even had breakfast already."

Greg hoped this deputy had not gotten a good look at his badge. Chicago's five-pointed star badge was distinct. The deputy looked young. Likely some part-timer getting experience while still in school. Hopefully, his inexperience would prevent him from asking for better identification.

Taking a gamble, Greg stepped into the kids' personal space. He answered by taking two steps to his left, giving Greg access to the door. Turning the knob on the door, Greg looked at the kid saying, "you think he will talk to me or tell me to get bent?"

"He seems friendly to me, sir. I bet he talks your ear off like he has been doing to Officer Thompson."

Before fully opening the door, Greg said, "Hope you're right."

Inside the room, a middle-aged man was sitting up in the lone hospital bed. A TV in the corner was tuned to a cooking channel. The man, Greg assumed to be Libertino, watched the television transfixed. Looking at the man, Greg guessed him to be about one hundred sixty pounds and just about five foot seven inches. Libertino's arms sat in his lap, holding the remote control. His biceps and forearms, while modest, looked like solid muscle.

"Hi, Detective Mike Radvich from St. Louis. Are you Libertino?"

Without even turning to look at Greg, "Si, but call me Bob."

"Okay, Bob. Mind if I ask a few questions?"

Bob's eyes darted towards Greg, then back to the television. "Si... I talk. Can we wait for episode to be over?"

The television was to Bob's right. The IV stood to the left of Bob's bed. Greg grabbed a chair and moved it to the left of Bob's bed, right next to the tubes running off the IV. Dangling next to the bed was a drug port, a section of tubing with a piece sticking out making like a letter Y. Greg stuck the needle of Heroin into the port, but did not push the plunger.

Finally, a commercial came. "Okay, what are we talking about, officer?"

"Recap me on everything you told Officer Thompson, please."

For ten minutes, Libertino explained his connection to Anthony DeRege and coming to America. Knowing Libertino had confessed everything to the local cops, Greg started pushing the drug out of the syringe into the IV tubes.

Chapter Fourteen

"What are you doing in so early?" Angie asked, seeing Stu walk past the dispatch center.

"Bob," Stu said, trying to figure out how to explain the mess his last few days had become. "Got a cop from St. Louis up to interview Bob. We agreed to meet here close to nine."

"Okay, but it's only seven. You have two hours before this guy is going to show up."

"I don't know how Bob is going to react to this other cop. Thought because I have a rapport with him, I should go talk to Bob first. Let him know this other cop will be with me."

Angie was looking at her dispatch screen. Stu could see on the screen an officer was out on a complaint of property damage. The officer was typing information into their squad car laptop which was now showing up on Angie's screen. "Interesting. So far you are like the only person he has talked to. You think he will say anything to this guy from St. Louis?"

"Don't know. Worth a try, right?"

"Just as long as you don't waste the guys drive up here from St. Louis."

"I paid for a few rounds of beer last night. That alone can't be a waste of a drive, right?"

Angie laughed at Stu's joke. Looking back at her screen, she typed a response to the officer at the property damage call. Looking back at Stu. "So far all I have been hearing is small snippets about this case with Bob. Someday soon, I expect you to sit down and give me the full story. Okay?"

"No problem. Although I bet the real story is a lot less interesting than the rumors."

Yawning, Stu felt like this last few days had been over a month long. It always seemed to go this way. Complex cases came in on his off days. Meaning he was working extra hours. Earning a few extra bucks in overtime was nice, considering the remodeling work he was doing. However, his body was not too happy. Money could not buy sleep.

Driving towards the hospital, Stu considered heading home to just lie back down. One more hour of sleep would help to make him feel human again. Then again, sometimes going back to bed for an extended nap made the exhaustion feel worse. Plus, it would take too long to change into something he could sleep in. Police style khaki cargo pants, bullet-proof vest and a polo shirt were not an ensemble made for sleeping. Not to mention the carbon fiber holster along with a handcuff and spare magazine case strapped to his belt. Reality was once he had everything taken off it would be time to put it all back to meet the St. Louis cop.

Reserved parking spots sat on the south side of the hospital by the emergence room. However, Stu was heading into the general area of the hospital near the center of the building. Parking around that entrance was just general visitor spots. Stu figured it was better to take a general spot than park down by the ER. Public perception was becoming something all officers were increasingly concerned with. Why take a reserved spot when his business was not actually an emergency?

Stu rarely walked into the main lobby of the hospital. It was odd walking into an expansive lobby versus the small secure entrance the ER had at night. The lobby was an offshoot of the building, two stories of open area filled with natural light from one hundred eighty degrees of windows. Nodding a hello to the people at the reception desk, Stu made his way to the main elevator.

Alone in the elevator, Stu closed his eyes, and leaned on the wall. This was going to be a long day. It was a scheduled night to work, so it would become a long night as well. He still had four shifts with the rookie officer Walker. As a training officer, it was not right for Stu to take off and pawn young Dana off on someone else. His plan was to introduce Mike to Bob, then see how their talk went. If they had a rapport Stu would excuse himself to get some sleep. Actually, the plan had been Deputy Chief Jefferson's idea, but Stu was happy to follow it.

An electronic chirp announced the elevator reached the second floor. Opening his eyes, Stu watched the doors open, then stepped out into the hall. Having been to Bob's room a few times he didn't need to look at the signage for directions. A nurse must have brought a stool over for the reserve deputy. He was sitting face locked into the screen of his iPhone.

Not even fully looking up from the video on his phone. "Hey Officer Thompson, how goes it this morning?"

"Fine, little tired, but will figure out a way to make it all day. How about you?"

"Oh, you know. Babysitting a hurt guy in the hospital, living the dream."

"It's a tough job but someone has to do it... So how did it go overnight?"

Pausing the video to actually make eye contact. "Okay I think. Guy who worked overnight didn't say much when I relieved him. I just came on at seven. Bob was already awake and having breakfast." The deputy looked back down at his phone. "Oh, and that guy from St. Louis came in about twenty minutes ago."

"Wait what?"

"I was told a cop from out of town was coming in today. Mike, I think he said his name was from St. Louis, right?"

Pointing at the door, Stu asked. "Mike is in there talking to Bob?"

The kid didn't even bother to look up at what Stu was pointing at. "Yeah."

"Alone, or was anyone else from Platteville PD with him?"

"Nope. Just him."

Grabbing the door handle. "Did you check his ID card? How do you know he is who he said he is?"

"He had a badge--"

Stu only half heard what the reserve deputy was saying. Pulling the door open, a wave of relief washed over Thompson seeing the cop he knew as Mike Radvich sitting next to Bob. "Detective Radvich, I thought the plan was for us to come here a little later in the morning?"

"I should ask you the same thing, Officer Thompson." Mike said as he stood up.

"I just wanted to talk to Bob first and let him know you were coming. Ya' know prevent a surprise that cou--" Before finishing his sentence Stu felt what was best described as a sledge hammer hit him in the chest. He didn't hear the gunshot. Before he could register what happened a second impact hammered the middle of his chest.

Confused, Stu saw Mike with a silver gun in his hand. Looking over towards Bob, he was still in his hospital bed and empty-handed. Instinct kicked in. Stu sidestepped to get out of the door frame while drawing his sidearm. A hospital recliner style chair stood to the right of the door. Without a thought, Stu moved behind it to put something between himself and the shooter. Problem was, he couldn't figure out who the shooter was.

Out of the corner of his eye, Stu saw the reserve deputy enter the room, weapon out. He fired off two shots that went wild toward Mike. Dropping to a knee Mike returned fire at the deputy. After three rounds at the deputy, Mike pointed his weapon at Stu and fired. Two rounds came through the chair Stu ducked behind and whizzed past his ear into the wall behind him.

Leaning out from the other side of the chair he had been looking from before Stu saw the deputy was lying on the ground. Blood poured out of his leg. Bob's bed was blocking his view of Mike. Every breath Stu took sent a wave of pain around his chest. Movement at the edge of the bed. Stu fired a round, but it struck the footboard of the bed. Mike popped up, aiming his gun over the top of the bed at Stu. Ducking down Stu made himself as small as possible behind the chair. Multiple rounds passed over his head into the wall.

Peeking out, Stu could see Mike ducked back behind the bed. Glancing at the bed, Stu noticed Bob was looking at the ceiling with wide, blank eyes. Bob's face looked like a dead person, but a slight rise in his chest said he was still breathing.

Stu could hear screaming outside the room from the hallway. He also heard a slide release. Mike had reloaded. He hoped someone was calling nine-one-one. If only he had grabbed a radio. Foolishly, he felt being in plain clothes a cell phone would be good enough for contacting the department. Trying to dig his phone out of a pocket seemed impractical while also trying to survive a gun fight.

Mike jumped up, holding a gun in each hand. Stu fired off two shots, then ducked back behind the chair. Again, the wall over his head exploded with rounds hitting it. This time the sound the of the gun fire moved. Mike was providing himself cover fire as he ran out of the room. Leaning out from the chair, Stu saw Mike exit the room. He took a shot at the fleeing gunman but missed.

Standing, Stu stumbled towards the door. Slowly approaching the doorframe Stu took steps sideways in what the SWAT guys called slicing the pie. With each breath, the searing pain in his chest increased. Looking out into the hall, Stu watched as Mike vanished into the stairwell.

His breath shallow Stu felt he was not getting enough air. He was sucking wind like a sprinter trying to run a marathon. Stu wanted to take a deeper breath, but the pain in his chest was too much. Blurry lines formed at the edge of his vision. Realizing he was about to pass out, Stu lowered himself to the floor.

A nurse runs up to Stu, asking if he is okay. Unable to get enough air to talk, all Stu could do for a reply was cough. Glancing at the deputy laying on the floor, Thompson could see blood gushing from the kid's leg. Pointing at the wound, he convinced the nurse to deal with that as a priority problem.

Other nurses rushed into the room. One is tying a makeshift tourniquet onto the deputy's leg. The extra pressure from the tourniquet looked to have slowed the bleeding. Someone had pulled a bed from some other room and they were loading the deputy up onto it. Stu heard a nurse talking about wheeling a shooting victim down to the ER.

"I don't think this guy is breathing!" Stu turned towards the voice. A nurse was standing next to Bob's bed. Forcing himself back to his feet, Stu took a few steps towards Bob. Something out of place caught his eye. A syringe hung from the tubes on Bob's bed. Two of the hospital staff were now checking Bob's vitals. "I got a pulse, but his heart rate is dropping off."

His breath was coming back, and the fog in his brain cleared. Stu looked at the needle in the IV and made a quick assumption. Thrusting a hand into his left leg cargo pocket, Stu pulled out a tube of Narcan. Chemical name Naloxone, a nose spray the cops and paramedics carried to reverse a heroin overdose.

Wheezing as he talked. "This guy works for a known heroin dealer. One reason we had a deputy sitting outside his room." Holding the Narcan out to the nurse and pointing at the syringe. "The guy who shot this place up was trying to murder him," Stu needed to pause for a few breaths before finishing, "by overdose."

Both nurses looked over Thompson's shoulder. Someone was standing behind him. Turning, Stu saw one of the attending doctors. The doctor must have caught what Stu said, as he nodded and pointed to the nurse. She took the spray and administered it to Bob.

"Officer," the doctor pointed to a chair by the window. "You better take a seat. It looks like you got shot."

Till this point Stu had been forcing himself not to look. Feeling compelled by the Doctor's statement Stu looked at his chest. He saw three holes in his shirt.

Chapter Fifteen

Hunched down behind the bed, Greg considered what to do next. He had initially shot at Officer Thompson with the gun Joey DeRege provided him. He thought he could pass it off as Libertino. It would be child's play to plant the gun on Libertino after the shooting was over.

Greg knew he hit Thompson, but the cop seemed to be in the fight still. More and more cops seemed to wear vests working plain clothes. Anti police protests and executions of cops on duty had officers around the country being more careful about personal safety. Thompson had to have seen him shoot the deputy.

That damn deputy he had come rushing into the room blasting away. Screaming into his radio microphone about shots fired while trying to control his weapon one handed. Dropping to his stomach to avoid the bullets, Greg returned fire. He did not know how many of his shots hit, but he knew one round slammed into the kid's upper right thigh. The kid was lying on the ground holding his leg as blood poured out. His gun was on the floor between the two men.

With the kid out of the fight, Greg only needed to worry about Officer Thompson. Time was not on his side. Backup was likely on the way. Greg needed to get out of the room fast. Glancing up at Libertino, he saw the man was already under the effects of the heroin. When he heard Thompson's voice in the hallway before coming in, Greg had pushed the plunger on the needle.

Libertino would be dead in short order with that amount of nearly pure heroin hitting his system. Greg just needed to get out of the room. Taking the silver gun in his left hand, he un-holstered his duty Glock in his right. Stu was behind the chair by the door. Pivoting to face the chair, Greg stood and fired off rounds. Left trigger, right trigger, left trigger, right trigger. He spaced out his shots between the two guns to keep the other cop's head down while rushing to the door.

Once in the hall, Greg sprinted to the stairs. Adrenaline filled his system. It felt as if he was running faster than he ever had. Down the stairs two at a time, he holstered his Glock. While trying to stuff the silver gun in his pants, it fell from his hands. In a moment of panic, Greg abandoned the gun provided to him by the mob and continued out the main floor door into the lobby.

Upstairs people had been panicking. Screams and ducking in the hallway. In the lobby, it surprised Greg to find people oblivious to what was happening a few feet overhead. The hospital must have good soundproofing. Forcing himself to walk, he made a beeline to the exit doors. His early arrival allowed him a parking spot in the second row.

Pulling out of the parking stall, Greg rolled down the windows. The faint warbling of sirens sounded in the distance. At the exit to the parking lot, Greg needed to decide. Turning to the right was a direct route to the highway. Turning to the left would bring him into the city. Cops expect someone making an escape trying to get to the highway to create the greatest distance from the crime scene quickly.

Turning left he drove into the city. Siren sounds were getting closer. Up ahead, Greg saw a big box hardware store. Signaling, he turned into the parking lot just as two squad cars buzzed past him on their way towards the hospital.

Finding a parking spot, he walked into the store. "Good Morning, sir. Have you seen this week's sales ad?"

"No, I don't get the paper anymore. Do you got a copy?"

"Sure do, here ya go."

Employees don't always remember the nice, average customers. It is always the jerks that stand out. Greg figured he better be friendly to the store greeter to fade into the background.

Walking around the store, he took some time to look at items he actually was thinking about getting for his apartment. Mainly a lightbulb for the shower that had a bluetooth speaker built into it. Something so a person could play music or a podcast on their phone yet hear the audio when getting ready in the morning. It was something one of the other detectives on his team kept talking about.

Walking around the store holding the lightbulb he stopped to admire some power tools. Looking at tools seemed like the generic guy thing to do. Eventually the tool area got boring so Greg made his way to the cheek out.

This store staffed only one cash register with a human. The store had half a dozen checkout lanes. Otherwise, there was a bank of eight registers labeled as self checkout. Just before entering the self checkout area, Greg stopped at a small refrigerator filled with energy drinks. Grabbing a drink, he then proceeded to the self checkout.

Walking back to his car holding a bluetooth light bulb and a caffeine drink in hand he felt it was safe to go toward the highway south of town. Not wanting to risk the drive past the hospital Greg went into town and then circled back down towards the highway.

Once outside the city limits, he pulled out one of his cell phones. On television, they always called them burner phones. He never heard that term actually used. Everyone he knew called them TracFones just like the brand name of the phones. After keying in a number from memory, he hit send.

"Yeah?"

"This is Greg. I need to talk to Joey."

"Hold on a second."

The sound of footsteps and some people talking came over the phone.

Joey DeRege's unmistakable voice came on the line, "Greg my friend. How are you enjoying Platteville?"

"It was a delightful town, but I am happy to say my time there is done."

"Oh... so fast. Is everything you needed to do done?"

"Can I talk freely on this line?"

"Maybe. But why take a chance? Come to the house. We can talk in person."

"Okay see you in less than an hour."

"I will make sure the boys know I am expecting you."

Pulling up the driveway, Greg once again had to admire the amazing house. Knowing Joey did not want him armed. Greg placed his sidearm under the driver seat before exiting the car. Walking toward the front door, Greg lifted his shirt, revealing the empty holster still clipped to his belt.

"Boss is expecting you." The guard said as he opened the door.

The great room was empty. Walking past the oversized leather couch, Greg made his way to the floor to ceiling windows. It was a peaceful view. A stream ran behind the house, cutting across part of the tree line at the edge of the mowed yard then made a dogleg turn disappearing down into the woods.

A slight creaking noise from the door hinge sounded behind him. Then footsteps on the wood floor approached. Glancing over his shoulder, Joey was coming towards him.

"You like the view?"

"Don't see trees and water like this in the city much."

Pointing at the stream. "If you go back into the woods about two hundred yards, there is a small gorge. That stream has a waterfall going into a pond, then continues down the length of the gorge."

"Sounds amazing."

"Oh, it is. Very peaceful. Kind of place a person can sit to escape the crazy world. We filmed a few porn scenes there as well. Girl goes skinny dipping, then a hiker stumbles on her type of scenarios. Some of our bestselling vids."

Greg was not sure what to say, so he just muttered a "hum."

Joey motioned for them to move over towards the couches. Taking a seat, Greg took a breath and set the folder next to him, away from Joey. He didn't know what to expect from Joey. Would this be some kind of grilling, or was the mobster just looking to hear the story? "So tell me has Libertino been taken care of?"

"I shot him up with all the heroin you gave me."

"That would be enough to kill anyone. I trust you were able to do it quietly?"

"Umm... there was a minor complication."

Joey cocked his head slightly sideways, much like some dogs will do when the humans are talking. "A complication?"

"I had to shoot two cops. Used the gun you gave me, but had to fire some rounds from my personal Glock."

"What the fuck? You got some real balls. I think my brother has underestimated your commitment to this family." Looking off in the distance for a second. "Wait... can the Platteville cops identify you? Track you back to Chicago? Or did you kill them too?"

"I might have killed the one. Not sure. Deputy sheriff, young looking kid, likely some kind of reserve or auxiliary deputy. Other one was a city cop. Hit him square in the chest, but I think he had on a vest. Hit him, think and move to cover."

"Okay. Did you leave us exposed here? Did you have to show ID to get into his room or anything?"

"Actually, I have the perfect alibi." Greg explained how when he arrived, the kid working dispatch assumed he was Detective Mike Radvich from St. Louis. "I untucked my shirt to hide my Chicago badge. It also somewhat covered my gun. Which some cops like to do when out of their jurisdiction to be a tad more incognito. The dispatcher introduced me to everyone as this Mike guy, so I never corrected him."

"Who the fuck is Mike from St. Louis?"

"The fingerprint that first alerted me the cops had Libertino was from a murder in St. Louis. When your brother first *recruited* me, he gave me some out-of-state case names. Asked if I could find out if there was evidence like prints or DNA and flag them in the system. My guess would be the cops in Platteville called down to St. Louis to talk about the case. Likely, the guys down there wanted to send someone up to talk to Libertino. Mike was who they were sending. I was lucky and got there first."

"Lucky indeed. But before killing him were you able to verify Libertino had not talked?"

Picking up the folder, Greg handed over copies of the investigative report. "The guy I met with. Dude I also shot in the vest. His report details his interview with Libertino. Apparently, the local cops all call him Bob for some dumb reason. Anyhow told a detailed story about killing a man in front of your brother and Anthony helping him escape the crime scene. Names you and explains the little spy game of chalks marks and dead drops. Cop's report didn't have details of the locations, but I got the feeling Libertino told him everything."

"Shit... and this cop lived, you said?"

"I know I hit him dead center of the chest. But no blood and he started shooting back, so he had to have on a vest."

"Why didn't you shoot him in the head?"

"He was kind of shooting back at me." Greg could not help but let a sarcastic tone drop into his voice. "He jumped behind some cover, so I never got a good direct shot at him. When I saw a chance to exit, I took it."

Joey picked up the report and read it over. Flipping back and over the pages a second time he shook his head. "I don't like this. That cop knows too much. I think you need to go back and make it so he can't talk anymore."

"Wait... what? You telling me to go kill him? He filed that report. The damage is done. At least Libertino can't talk anymore, so there is nothing to substantiate what this officer says."

"Like you said there are likely details missing from this report. Libertino told him more. If he is gone, any extra details are gone with him."

Chapter Sixteen

Sirens in the background signaled backup was on the way. A nurse walked Stu to the hospital room one door down from Bob's. Guiding him to the bed, she started cutting his clothing off. First rule of emergency medicine is to find all the injuries. Just because blood was not pouring out did not mean he did not have a bullet hole some place.

An increasing level of pain was settling into his chest. The rush of the moment was washing off. Stu knew he was hurt, but felt confident it was not too bad.

After cutting his polo shirt off, she left his vest in place. Looking around his arms, shoulder, and stomach. "Do you feel any pain?"

"Yeah… a pressure on my chest. Maybe a little stinging sensation over to the left side, but still in the chest area."

"Okay. I don't see anything leaking out. The vest likely saved you. Doc said to keep it on you till you're in the ER. Just needed to do an initial assessment before I roll you down."

Talking had hurt, so Stu simply gave her a thumbs up.

———

As the hospital bed moved down the hall into the emergency room, Stu closed his eyes. The pain had leveled off, but each breath caused a spike of agony. He was afraid something was wrong. Had a round pierced into his body? Could the impacts of the bullets ruptured internal organs?

"Male late twenties with gunshot wounds to the chest. He had on a police vest and the rounds do not appear to have penetrated. Attending upstairs asked that I leave the vest on him till we got down here." The nurse's voice was cool and professional. She then listed off the numbers she had taken for Stu's heart rate and blood pressure before moving down to the ER.

A failure voice followed after the Nurse's. "Stu, is that you?"

"Yeah." Stu still had his eyes closed. It took him a second to place the voice. Doctor Sherbahn was one of the primary physicians who staffed the emergency room full time. In such a modestly sized town, the hospital could not support a complete complement of full-time emergency room doctors. A handful of staff worked regularly at Platteville's ER, supplemented by limited term or part-time contract workers. Junior doctors fresh out of medical school looking to pick up an extra paycheck to go towards student loan debt.

"Can you tell me about any pain?"

"Pressure across my whole chest. Bit of a sting to the left side. Only feel the sting as I breathe in."

"Alright. I am going to take this vest off you and then we will get your tee-shirt off."

The bed stopped rolling. Stu felt a little vibration in the bed as they kicked the wheel locks in. When his eyes were closed, the pain just felt less, so he kept them shut. A slight jostle and the sound of velcro releasing followed by the feeling of the front of his vest being plucked away. With his next breath, the sting in his chest eased.

"Ahh." Stu vocalized the relief he was feeling.

"Officer, is there something wrong?" Dr. Sherbahn asked.

Stu had not realized his little vocalization had been audible to others. "Yeah. When you lifted away my vest, that sting I was feeling almost went away."

"Well, I can see why. Take a look here at the inside of your vest."

Opening his eyes Stu saw the familiar dark blue outline of his vest carrier. The warn off label and lack of velcro tabs told Stu he was looking at the inside part of the vest. An area that would be on the left side of his chest had a deformity to it. Not a hole, but the fabric pushed out noticeably.

"Look here at this bit," Dr. Sherbahn was pointing at something near the deformity. "One of the bullets must have disintegrated into shards of metal. One of them cut its way though, allowing this little barb to poke you."

Focusing on where the doctor's finger pointed, Stu saw a little chunk of copper colored metal sticking from the fabric. Motioning for the doctor to hand over the vest, Stu looked at it closer. Turning, he looked at the outside face. Dead center of the vest were two side-by-side holes. A titanium trauma sat in the middle of many modern vests. Lucky Stu's vest had the hard plate. A third hole was a few inches to the left, at the edge of the plate. Likely that round had nicked the edge of the plate, shattering it. The copper jacket surrounding the lead bullet became the stinger that gave Stu such pain.

Taking the vest back, Dr. Sherbahn pointed at Stu's undershirt. Without needing anymore prompting, an ER nurse Stu didn't recognize started cutting the fabric.

"Looks good, Stu. You got a large contusion over the sternum. A second smaller one to the upper left pectoral, which includes a small incised wound." Turning to the nurse. "We are going to want to get that wound cleaned out. Set him up with an x-ray to make sure no metal slipped inside there. Also, get images of the full rib cage. I need to ensure nothing is cracked."

"Right away doctor."

Turning towards Stu. "It might be a few minutes before we get you over to x-ray. Let us know if you need anything for the pain."

Looking up at the ceiling tiles, Stu contemplated the chain of events leading to his being in the ER bed today. That chain lead all the way back to high school. He had made it known to his guidance counselor that police work was an interest. She introduced him to the police school liaison officer, who arranged a ride-along with a regular uniformed officer. Taking that opportunity to ride with an actual officer cemented with Stu his desire to become a cop. College classes, an internship, and the police academy all were his natural path.

Joining the Platteville Police was not his first choice. His hometown, a suburb outside of Green Bay, had always been his dream. When he graduated, that dream department was not hiring. Platteville was. Stu's dad convinced him it was better to have a job, even if not at the dream department. Versus having a dead-end part-time gig hoping the dream department would hire before his student loans went into default.

A week after he started at Platteville his dream department started accepting applications. If he had held out for that process, would he have gotten that job? Would he be lying in a hospital bed shot? Self loathing and self doubt were not his normal style. However, given his current situation, allowing a little doubt about life choices was not unheard of.

"Thompson, you okay?"

Stu snapped out of his daydream. Deputy Chief Jefferson stood at the side of his bed. "Been better sir." The nurse had already cleaned the area around the small hole in his chest and taped a chunk of gauze over it. The gauze was a bright shade of red and a small trickle of blood made a thin line down his side.

"You sure?" DC Jefferson pointed at the bloody gauze.

"Yeah, just an overgrown scratch. Think I overheard something about needing a few stitches for it. But they will not close it until after I have a few x-rays. Need to make sure no bones are broken and no little shards of metal are stuck in my chest."

"Look I know you have a lot of stuff going on in your head, but I got to ask a question or two."

"No problem. I know how the system works."

"Okay... the guy who did the shooting, was it that detective Radvich person who came up to meet with you?"

"Yes."

"Was there anyone else with him? Any other suspects we need to be aware of?"

"No. He came last night and helped me with the consent search at Bob's apartment. We planned to talk to Bob together today. I came in early to let Bob know I was going to have someone else with me. Walked into the room and Mike was already in the room."

"Just to clarify... Mike was the one who shot at you?"

"Yes. He was holding a silver gun. Later, he had two. The silver gun and what looked like a Glock."

"You returned fire at him?"

"Ye...yes." Until asked Stu had not thought about the fact he had shot at someone. Statistically speaking, few cops ever pull the trigger on their guns other than at the shooting range. He had been in a true gun battle. Not only had he been shot, but he had aimed at someone else and returned fire.

"Did you hit this guy? Is there a chance we have an injured person some place needing medical aid?"

"I don't think so. I ducked for cover, and he was behind cover as well. Not to mention when he had two guns and was dumping out suppressive fire."

DC Jefferson set a reassuring hand on Stu's shoulder. "You did good. The important thing is you are still alive and from what I got upstairs you likely saved Bob's life."

"How about the deputy?"

"Don't know much. He is in surgery. Took two in the vest but also one in the upper thigh. The fact he was still alive when he got down here means the femoral artery likely was not hit. But till he is out of surgery we won't know much."

Stu felt a wave of nausea wash over him. Not only had he escaped death, two other people had almost died. Reality had a way of hitting a person in the gut as reality set in. The shooter was gone; the scene was secure. He and the other two victims were getting medical aid. For all intents and purposes, the excitement was over. Everything happened so fast he had little time to think. The shooter was gone. Now he had time to think. The shooter was gone...

"Sir, we need to stop that Mike guy. Is there an ATL out for him?" ATL, shorthand for Attempt To Locate.

"That was one thing we needed for you to fill us in on. When you met this guy last night. What was he driving?"

"Never saw his car. I think he had parked in the public lot on third street. We went to Bob's place, came back to the PD and then walked up to get a beer. After having a few drinks, walked back to the PD. As I headed towards my car, he was heading in the lot's direction. But I don't recall seeing him jump in a car."

"Hmmm... okay... when you were talking did he happen to say what hotel he was staying at? Maybe they will have his vehicle info on the room registration."

Stu had to close his eyes to think for a second. When they were at the bar, Mike made a comment about his hotel. "I am not fully sure, but I think he was at the Country 7."

"That will be a start. We only have a handful of places in town to stay, so if that does not pan out officers will have to stop at all of them."

The nurse popped her head back into the room. "Excuse me. We need to take him to x-ray now."

"Oh sorry. Don't let me stop you from helping my officer here."

As she walked closer to the bed, the nurse pointed towards Stu's hip. "Are you able to take the gun from him? With some images we need to get, that might not be the best thing to have on."

Stu's holster for plain clothes was a paddle style one made by Fobus. A plastic composite that tucked into the pants but also had little hooks to pinch his belt. With a quick little twist of the wrist, Stu pulled the holster off and handed it along with his gun over to the deputy chief. "Here sir. I am sure it needs to be packaged as evidence anyhow. Crime lab will need to test it against any rounds recovered in the walls I shot at to help in reconstructing the scene."

"Thanks Stu. I will be here at the hospital most of the day I imagine. Will be back to check on you in a bit."

Chapter Seventeen

Greg took his time driving back up to Platteville. After the shootout, he had gotten down to the DeRege house as fast as possible. He was in no hurry to return to the city. Normally he would have music streaming from his phone. Instead, he was listening to local radio.

Just North of the gas station where he met the cop on his last drive towards Platteville Greg heard what he was hoping to hear. "Breaking news reports coming from Platteville indicate the hospital is still on lock down after a shooting. Police are not releasing much information." The radio DJ paused ever so briefly adding a dramatic effect to the news report. "Suspect details are sketchy at this time. However, the police say they are looking for a person thought to be from Missouri. No vehicle description is available. If anyone in the public has information, please contact the Platteville police at—"

Good Greg was still somewhat anonymous in the commission of this crime. Their assumption he was this cop from St. Louis was still holding up. It would not hold up for long. In the shooting's chaotic aftermath, they would focus on the injured cops and clearing the building. Make sure the active shooter was gone and not hiding in the basement some place. Once the scene had settled, an early call would be to the St. Louis police to figure out why their cop went rogue.

The call would have some bickering back and forth, but eventually the folks on the phone would realize someone had been faking the role of Officer Radvich. Once his ruse was figured out, the cops in Platteville would review the footage from the security cameras Greg noticed outside and in the police station.

Would this small potato department have access to facial recognition software? Greg knew the software was not as ubiquitous as television cop shows made it out to be. It was, however, out there. If this case had enough heat on it and some local cop had a buddy at the FBI, a favor could be called.

Knowing he was going to be doing something nefarious, Greg has kept his head down. He avoided the cameras as he made sure to never fully look face on at the camera. Still, the Platteville officers would have some images of a person to be looking out for. They would also pass these images on to other agencies in an attempt to locate.

He hated the idea, but Greg would have to change his look. In the next town, Cuba City, the highway was the main street right through the main downtown area. Passing a chain grocery store location, Greg signaled and turned into the parking lot.

For a small town grocery store, it was decent sized and well stocked. It did not have an organic nor gluten-free section but he imagined in a town such as this few people were as concerned with those diets. The few people who ate that way by choice or medical condition likely traveled for their shopping needs.

One small aisle had the heath and beauty aids. A very limited selection of deodorants, shaving supplies and other hygiene products. In the middle of the aisle Greg found the hair care products. They stocked two shelves with the common colors of hair dye. Blonde was the logical pick Greg guessed. Right now, he was a brownish red color. *If I go lighter, it will be easier to dye it back to something close to my natural color in a few days.*

He looked over the options, trying to figure out what would work best for his natural coloring. After a minute, he realized how clueless as a man he was about such things as hair coloring. Picking up a light blonde color he walked towards the checkout. *Once I get back to Chicago, I will make an appointment at a salon to have a professional make my hair look right again.*

Hungry, Greg took a lap past the deli to snag a pre-made ham sandwich. Standing at the checkout, he grabbed a bottle of coke from a little display cooler and a snack size bag of chips off a hook above the magazines.

Setting his purchases on the conveyor belt, the chaser gave Greg a brief sideways glance. He was sure she saw all kinds of odd combinations of things people buy. Lunch and hair dye could not be the oddest but still not an everyday normal.

"Wife texted me. Said something about roots showing and to get her this box when I was out today."

The clerk nodded her head. "Lucky woman. Most husbands would pick the wrong box."

"Oh, she knows me. She was specific. Revlon, Natural Blonde number four. Hard to mess it up when there is even a number guide."

She told Greg the total and had handed over cash. "You have a single brother?"

"No, Why?"

"Too bad. You're kind of cute and it sounds like your mom raised you to treat a woman right. Wishful thinking. Trying to find a decent man, ya' know."

She handed back his change. Greg took a quick look at her name tag. "Thanks Kendra." Greg felt embarrassed by her semi flirtation. Had he not been feeling stressed of the day's events Greg might have flirted back. Instead, he grabbed the bag of his purchases and walked to the parking lot.

Greg had not actually checked out of the hotel when he left in the morning. Just emptied the room and left a key on the nightstand. More and more chain hotels were allowing guests to just leave versus stopping at the front desk for a formal checkout. In the age of swipe cards, there was no need or expectation to return physical keys as in the past.

When he left, Greg had kept one key just in case. Parking at the hotel, he went inside and made his way back to the room he slept in the night before. He had checked in for a few days but only used one night. Sliding the key in the lock, the light turned green, showing he still had access.

Tossing his duffle bag on the bed, Greg looked in the mirror. He looked like a cop. Cargo pants and an Under Armour polo shirt. That would have to change. Opening the duffle bag, he pulled out jeans.

After reading the instructions on the hair dye, he stripped down and walked to the bathroom. Following the directions, Greg mixed the chemicals and, wearing the included gloves, applied the solution to his hair. According to the instructions, he needed to wait about twenty minutes, so he went back out to the room and clicked on the television.

Midday had little that Greg found interesting. So he selected the headline news channel. The anchor was droning on about some new policy being proposed by the President. After the commercial break, they did a weather forecast to detail travel delays at airports along the southern coast. Once the weather was done, they had an update about the shooting at the Platteville hospital.

"Police have ended the lockdown on the hospital in Wisconsin after an early morning shooting. We take you to an update recorded by a local affiliate just a few minutes ago."

The image shifted to a male who looked to be in his early thirties. "Officials in Platteville, Wisconsin are still being tight lipped about what took place this morning. Witness report hearing gun fire before the building was put on lockdown. During the lockdown, the Emergency Room remained open but isolated from the rest of the hospital. Officers from multiple local agencies cleared the hospital but were unable to locate the gunmen. Once the hospital was cleared, it was reopened for routine business. Witnesses say a room on the second floor is blocked off with crime scene tape."

The images on the screen were just distance shots of squads flanked around the hospital, light bars blinking. A few cops milled about talking and trying not to look directly at the cameras filming from across the street. With no real action to show, the image jumped back to the reporter standing with the hospital over his left shoulder.

"An official statement from the police chief says two officers were hurt and are in surgery. Both are expected to survive. Names are not being released at this time. Suspect information will be released at a press conference scheduled for one in the afternoon after confirming information with an outside agency. What that means we don't know yet. This is Evan Koval reporting on the scene in Platteville for..."

Greg felt relief he had not killed Officer Thompson and the deputy. He was many things, but a cop killer was not one. At the time, it was self preservation. All instinct and no real thought. Joey had ordered him to now kill the officer, and Greg was feeling conflicted. The next time it would not be instinct however there would still be a measure of self preservation.

Standing back up and walking to the bathroom, Greg started the shower. Once the water was warm, he jumped in and started rinsing the chemicals from his hair. A conditioner had to also be applied and left in for about two minutes before rinsing it off.

The hot water and steam felt good. Sitting on the floor of the shower, Greg let the steam envelop him. The heat relaxed his muscles. Until he had been in the warm water, he didn't realize how the stress of the morning had tightened everything up. It felt like he had been through a brutal workout.

Once the water started to chill, he stood and turned off the shower. Drying off, he looked in the mirror. Do blondes actually have more fun? The hair color would not fool close friends. A stranger who he had limited contact with should not notice who he was right away.

The news reporter said the officer was in surgery. It was likely then they would not discharge the cop from the hospital for a few days. That could make Greg's job easy and hard. Easy because he would not have to figure out where this cop lived to hunt him down. Hard because the hospital would likely have tightened security. Greg would not be walking right into the cop's room like he had Libertino's room this morning.

Returning to the main room, the news had cycled back to the story of the shooting. Like many things on the cable news channels, they just replayed the pre recorded broadcast he saw before getting into the shower. It was only a quarter after noon. The press conference was not for another hour.

He grabbed his laptop from his backpack and sat at the small table in the far corner of the room. Television still on, he listened halfheartedly to the other headlines of the day. Scanning the headline lines of Google News, he checked to see if any of the other news outlets had scooped a better story. Hoping someone inside the PD had tipped off a reporter as an anonymous source Greg read over a few stories.

Nothing much differed from story to story. One news outlet had gotten a quote from a person visiting the hospital. Another had a shaky cell phone video showing people running out of the hospital. A third one had a quote from a patient in the ER at the time they rolled the officers past. That site also shared the video from the other webpage linking back to their story.

All the new feeds seemed to do was rehash variations of the same story. Many even updated theirs to offer content from other pages with links to the original source. After a few minutes Greg felt he was making circles looking at stories linking to others, that linked to others that all linked back to each other at some point.

Changing gears, Greg typed in the name of Officer Stuart Thompson into Google. The list of stories was not long. It was time to learn a bit more about this cop. The cop Joey ordered Greg to silence.

Chapter Eighteen

"This is an obvious example of two guys with a history that boiled over in public. Best part, someone had their cell phone out recording so we get to see it."

"You know JS, I wonder if one of these guys is dating the other guy's ex-wife."

Officer Mike Radvich was on the last stretch of his drive, crossing the state of Iowa. The drive up from St. Louis was just over five hours. North up Interstates 55 and 74 through Illinois till crossing into Iowa. Then highway 61 north till linking up with 151 just shy of the Wisconsin border.

To entertain himself, Mike was listening to various podcasts. At the start of his trip, it was primarily some motivational self help shows. Now he was needing some humor to keep himself awake. His go to funny podcast was hosted by a police officer and a paramedic from northern California. The two men always had great insights on public safety news. Also, because of social media rules, they two did not use their names, just their initials.

This week they were talking about a police officer and EMT who had gotten into a physical altercation responding to a late night bar fight. One person in the bar fight had taken a serious injury but was trying to fight the medical workers. So the police pulled out a TASER. One EMT blocked the officer from using the TASER, fearing the shock would cause an already injured person more injury. Quickly, the cop and medic were at odds. Resulting in a second fight breaking out, when the EMT punched the officer.

Officer Radvich had seen the same scene a few times. Although never to the point of cops and EMTs getting into a fight. Typically, it ended with the cops just looking at the EMTs asking what they should do.

"I bet you are right about someone dating the ex of someone else. Regardless MC we both agree this was nothing more than two guys measuring their junk to see who has the longest tool. And once the cameras rolled, both guys ended up on the *interweb* looking like tools."

Mike could not help but to shake his head in disbelief. They were right. Sometimes people in public safety don't get along. In the age of cell phone cameras uploading videos on YouTube, it was very easy for a personal grudge to become a public embarrassment.

The two pod casters moved on to a new topic dealing with a funny event that happened on shift. It was a story about a court case and body camera footage. This story had Mike laughing out loud thinking about some videos officers he works with had recorded. The humor of these two hosts kept Mike perked up awake for the final push of the drive.

Pulling to the top of the ramp, it surprised Mike to see he was still out on a county road. This was the first exit for Platteville, but the highway was still some ways from the city. He could see some tall buildings that looked like dorms sticking up from a tree line in the distance.

His GPS announced to keep on this current road for just under a mile before his next turn. The road sloped down and rounded a small hill. Rounding the corner, Mike saw a commercial district just appear. Like the hillside was a curtain blocking the view of the city's limits. A string of fast-food joints, gas stations, and family restaurants stretched from the hill to the upcoming intersection he was to turn at.

It was just before one in the afternoon. Mike had left home just after seven in the morning. He had planned to be on the road sooner, his morning it just did not work out that way. Stopping for gas and for food had added a little time to his drive.

The hotel listed check in after three. In Mike's experience, many hotels allowed checking in nearly anytime after about one. He did not feel like pushing his luck, so opted to head up to the police station first. He figured getting a rundown from the officer on the case before checking into his room would be a good use of time. Hopefully, this officer Thompson guy could even get him face-to-face with the mysterious killer.

Driving up Water street Mike found the city to be beautiful. It was built into a hillside running up out of a valley. What he could only assume to be limestone outcroppings added natural barriers between business parking lots that sat just a few feet above each other. The road had a steady incline, but the shops on the street zigzagged up the hill like stairs. It gave a cool, eccentric ascetic detective Radvich had never seen before.

Turning onto the aptly named Main Street, Mike found himself on a gentler incline of a road. A historic looking area with buildings that dated back to the late 1800s yet filled with modern businesses. Quickly the GPS had him turning up a one-way street, and he was at his destination.

Just a block away from the historic buildings, the Police station looked like new construction. Brick and glass, it was an attractive building but yet had all the flair of government utilitarian contractors. When looking at the building, they offset the main entrance to the left side. A large amount of green space filled with trees made the department look inviting to the Detective from an urban concert landscape.

On the doors, stenciled hours showed the lobby was open to walk-in customers. After hours, visitors had a large red button to press. Walking into the lobby, Mike found the department to have a warm, inviting feel. There was still bulletproof glass separating the lobby from the front desk, but the design did not call attention to how thick that glass was.

"Hi, how can I help you?" A middle-aged woman asked from behind the glass. A small speaker next to the window amplified her voice.

"I have an appointment with Stu Thompson, err... Detective Thompson."

"You have an appointment?"

"Well, not an appointment per se, but he was expecting me here today."

"Okay, mind if I get your name?" She put on an uncomfortable smile.

"Sure, Detective Mike Radvich, St. Louis Police."

"Wait here" She rushed out the door of her work area out of sight.

Mike turned to look at the lobby. A few plaques on the wall to commemorate the achievements of the little league teams sponsored by the police. A public announcement board listing public meetings to be held in the meeting room behind the double doors on the other side of the lobby. Mike was interrupted while reading the agenda for the upcoming police and fire commission meeting.

"Hands up now!"

Turning, Officer Radvich saw two officers in the doorway next to the reception desk. One had a gun out the other had a TASER. Mike out of instinct put his hands up. "Hey guys. I am one of you. Got my badge if you want to see it."

"Shut up and keep your hands in the air," yelled the cop with the gun.

Mike did as was told, but felt the need to say. "Hey brother, I am a cop. Let me show you my badge." With little thought, Mike dropped his hand to reach for his wallet. Before getting into touch with his billfold, Mike felt a pair of sharp pricks in his chest and abdomen. Fifty-thousand volts disrupting all his muscle activity immediately followed the pricks.

Falling to the floor Detective Radvich could only wonder what was going on. Intellectually, he knew he was being hit with the TASER, but could not figure out why. As the ground rushed towards his face, he tried to put his hands out to stop the fall, but the electrical shock prevented him from moving any limbs.

Slamming into the ground, he felt his left cheek bounce off the tile flooring. Small miracle he did not land nose first. The officers swarmed him. Mike could hear the click, click, click of the TASER pulse. Five seconds felt like an eternity. Then the clicking ended and he no longer felt the electrical voltage. He still could not move as one officer took up a position over him, placing a knee on Mike's left shoulder. That officer had hold of Mike's left arm and was moving into a handcuffing position.

The other officer knelt down on Mike's right side, scooping up his right arm. He wanted to resist, but reason overcame the knee jerk reaction of fighting cops. These guys already had him in a position of compliance. They won the fight. Any attempt to break away would only result in an elevation in using force, which would lead to an injury.

Once the cuffs were on, the officers asked Mike if he was OK. It seemed an odd move, but showed a level of professionalism. Their suspect was in custody, so now they wanted to make sure they did not hurt him by getting him under control.

"Yeah... but you are making a mistake treating me like this."

The officer to his left answered. "You shot two cops. How should we treat you?" The officer didn't give Mike a chance to respond. "I am going to search for you. Do you have any weapons on you?"

"Yes, duty pistol on my right hip but my badge is also in my right back pocket."

"I don't care about your badge. Cop shooting other cops is not cool." The officer patted Mike down very precisely. Mike's duty weapon was removed, along with his wallet and cell phone. "Are you able to stand up?"

"Sure."

The officer helped Mike to sit, then directed him to his knees and finally to a standing position. Once on his feet, the needle probes from the TASER were plucked from Mike's body. Again, Mike was asked if he was okay.

"I think so. Is there any blood coming from where the darts hit?"

"Not that I can see," said the officer with a name tag reading Noris. "Would you like us to call for an ambulance? Would you like for an EMT to look you over?"

Mike grunted and shook his head "no". Noris motioned towards the doorway by the reception desk. Walking into the nonpublic area of the police department, they led Mike to an interview room. Much like the interview rooms he took suspects to it had few movable pieces of furniture. Precast concrete made up much of the room. Two stools and a simple tabletop between the stools.

One of the other officers took Mike's handcuffs off. Noris pointed at the stool further from the door. Mike sat as the non-verbal cue told him to.

"Before I ask any questions, I must say it takes some monster balls to come back here. Seriously, shoot a cop and walk right into the lobby of his department. You got some low hanging bass nuts my man."

Taken aback, all Mike could say was, "I didn't do it."

"Okay, well before we talk about what you did and did not do I need to read you, your rights." Noris, who Mike also noticed had sergeant stripes on his shirt read the so-called Miranda warning from a printed form. After reading the statement over, he asked if Mike understood his rights.

"Yes, I understand them."

"Good. Can you check the box here showing YES and then initial the line behind it?"

Mike did as instructed.

"Understanding these rights, are you willing to answer questions without a lawyer?"

"For now, I will talk to you, yes, but the second this thing feels like it is going sideways I will ask for a lawyer."

"Good. Again, please check the box and initial the line. Then also can you sign the bottom of the page?"

Mike did as instructed again.

Before he could say anything a knock at the door interrupted Noris. In walked a middle-aged woman with dark reddish hair. She was in khaki cargo pants and a gray polo. "Detective Herrisch. Perfect timing. I would like to introduce you to Detective Mike Radvich from the St. Louis police." Turning towards Mike, "Our detective here will take over talking to you."

Chapter Nineteen

Stu sat propping himself up on his elbow in the hospital bed as Deputy Chief Jefferson came back into the room. The hospital staff had moved Officer Thompson from a trauma room to a general examination room. Eavesdropping on some of the chatter, Stu assumed he would be sent home later today.

"How you feeling?"

"Only hurts when I breathe, but hurts a bit more when I am talking."

The deputy chief cracked a smile. "Guess I can't tell you to stop breathing. As for talking, try to do as little as possible yet, there are a few things we need to talk about."

"Sure boss." Stu grabbed the control for the bed to adjust the bed into a fully seated position.

"Sorry, it has taken me a bit to get back to you. Things have been a little crazy as you can imagine. It took a bit longer than we expected to clear the building. We had an ATL out for an unknown car with Missouri plates driven by this Mike Radvich."

"Have you called St. Louis PD?"

"Not yet. Hate to say it but I have been scared to call them."

Stu was taken aback by his supervisor's comment. "Scared? Why?"

Pointing at a chair in the room, the Deputy Chief asked permission to sit. Stu nodded, and Jefferson took a seat at the leading edge. "You know how it is. Cops defend cops. I call them. They are going to say one of their own could not have done it. Then they will call him on his cell and tell him to find a spot to lay low and hide out."

"I don't know sir. If you got a call, one of us was suspected of shooting a cop. Would you protect the officer that way? Tell them to lie low."

The Deputy Chief pondered the idea for a second. "I guess not. But I would call the officer to tell them to turn themselves in. Which would tip the officer off they should go into hiding. Ben Graystock had little warning about what you suspected him of doing and yet look how he vanished for half a year."

Graystock was a former Platteville police officer who had become a vigilante, burning down the homes of drug dealers. He had become disenchanted when one dealer, Avery Spade, was unable to ever be arrested. Ben hatched a plan to burn his house, thinking the fire would expose Avery's basement meth lab. The fire did too much damage. So Ben set more fires and even killed a young man accidentally.

At first, the assumption had been a drug war between rival dealers. Thompson, as a fire investigator, ended up connecting some dots to figure out his co-worker was responsible. Inadvertently, Thompson tipped Ben off, and he was able to be on the run for six months before being captured.

It was easy for Stu to see why Jefferson was being slow to call St. Louis. Better to hope the suspect was caught and in custody than give him a chance to go on the run. Although with a vague ATL, the chance of finding the suspect was slim. Stu was doing the math in his head, and realized the suspect could almost be back in the St. Louis area by now.

"So are you getting ready to call?"

"Yes, but I need my ducks in a row. I can't just call down there and make an accusation about their officer without the story being solid. You need to walk me through the last twenty four hours again."

Thompson explained how he met the other officer in the dispatch center and they did the search of Bob's apartment. In this rendition of the story, Stu went into detail about taking the officer out for pizza and some beers. Then getting up early to talk to Bob. He explained he did not want to surprise Bob with this out-of-town cop. But when he arrived the other cop was already in the room and next thing he knew there was shooting.

"You are sure the person who shot you was the officer from the night before?"

"One-hundred percent sure. We talked for a long time. His face was the same. He looked me in the eye as he shot me. I don't think I will ever forget that moment. Don't know if I want to remember it, but can't forget it."

"I can't imagine. Sorry to ask, but they will ask this of me. Did you check his ID or see his badge?"

Stu sat thinking for a moment. Replayed the events in his mind. "I don't know."

"What do you mean you don't know? If someone walks into the PD claiming to be a cop from out of town, we don't just take their word for it. Would you expect to waltz into some other department and have them roll out the red carpet without verifying who you say you are?"

Letting out a small sigh of frustration caused Stu to wince in pain. "No sir. It is just that when I met the guy, he was sitting in dispatch talking to Carl. When I got introduced to the guy, I may have assumed Carl checked his credentials before allowing him to sit in the comm center."

Jefferson's shoulders slumped. Stu knew he had made a good point. "Okay, that is a reasonable assumption to make. We might need to get Carl on the phone and find out if he checked the guy out." The deputy chief looked up at the ceiling and rolled his eyes. "God, I hope that kid did not screw up again."

Before Stu could say anything the radio the Deputy Chief was holding chirped out a voice. "P15 to P2."

"Go for P2."

"Boss, you may want to start heading back towards the police department. We just had that officer from Missouri walk into the lobby of the police department. Herrisch has him in the back getting a statement."

Stu and the deputy chief exchanged some quizzical glances.

"Are you free for a phone call?"

"10-4 boss, I am in dispatch."

After setting the portable radio on the table next to the hospital bed, Deputy Chief Jefferson fished his cell phone from his front pants pocket. After tapping on the screen, he held the device to his ear.

Stu could hear the muffled sound of the ring and someone pick up. The voice on the other end sounded male, like that of Sgt. Noris, radio call sign P15. Stu, however, could not make out exact words.

"Are you telling me that our suspect just walked into the PD?"

The muffled voice of Sgt. Noris took on an excited tone.

"So you have this guy in custody and you physically are holding his wallet in your hand."

This time Stu could make out the "yes" coming from Noris.

"What is the exact name on his id? Is it the same on the driver's license, department identification and all the credit cards?"

More chatter from the other end of the phone that Stu could not fully make out.

Jefferson held the phone away from his face. Looking at Stu. "Guy showed up at the PD, name is Micheal K. Radvich, detective from St. Louis."

"Yeah, that is the guy I talked to on the phone and said he was coming to town. That was the name the guy used who I met with and who shot me a few hours ago."

Speaking back into the phone. "Keep him in the interview room. Even if he lawyers up. Hold on to him before heading up to jail. We will be there ASAP. Got it?" More chatter on the other end of the phone. Jefferson said his goodbye and then hung up. Looking at Stu. "Hit that nurse call button. We need to get you out of here sooner rather than later."

Confused, "What? Why, what good can I do?"

"I want you to look at this guy. Verify if it is the dude who shot you."

"Why not have a photo taken and emailed to us?"

"I don't want any confusion from looking at a low-resolution image on a cell phone screen. If the doc will release you we need to have you ID this guy in custody."

Stu hit the call button and offered a half ass smile at his boss. Less than a minute later a nurse came in. "Is there a problem?"

Deputy Chief Jefferson spoke before Officer Thompson could. "Something has come up. It is important I get this officer back to the police station as soon as possible. We were hoping the doctor could give him a final once over and then discharge him."

Rolling her eyes, the nurse said she would be back and stomped out of the exam room.

Jefferson seemed uncomfortable in the silence. He looked around the room. Finally he asked. "Why do you think this guy would come back and walk into our lobby?"

"I was thinking about that, as you were on the phone. My best guess is that he was afraid someone would kill him. Think about it. He shot cops. The ATL said he is armed and had tried to kill some LEOs. If he got pulled over by the wrong trooper, it could be shoot first and ask questions later."

"Very true. Self-preservation can be a powerful influence on folks. But why not just go into hiding and hope to never be contacted by any cops?"

Leaning back looking up at the ceiling, Stu thought about the question. "It seems there is some kind of Mob involvement. Bob was talking about meeting folks in Italy. This cop might be dirty. Maybe he knows he did not kill anyone. Turn himself in and what... he does only a handful years in prison. If he keeps his mouth closed about who his boss is, maybe there is a massive payday after he gets out."

"You thinking he came into the police department playing some long game?"

"Yeah. I bet he thinks he killed Bob. Mission accomplished, right? I had agreed to meet him later in the morning. His plan was to sneak in, shoot Bob up with dope to cause an OD death, then slip away. I came in at the wrong time. He didn't think I would come see Bob before our arranged meeting time. Shooting at me and the deputy was just an impulse."

Deputy Chief Jefferson nodded his agreement with Stu's theory. "So this guy thinks he did what he was asked to do. Which was killing Bob. Getting in a shootout with you was a fuckup. Dumb luck he gets away, but once things cool down, he realized there was no long-term escape. But wait a second... if he tried to murder Bob he could be looking at a long time in prison."

"We don't have solid proof he did it. No one saw him put the needle in Bob's arm. He could raise a reasonable doubt on several levels with both Bob and the shootings. If he has a good lawyer, he takes a plea deal and gets some cakewalk sentence. I bet he already talked to whoever pulls his strings, and they put him in touch with a lawyer. That attorney told him what to do and already is setting the groundwork so he can end up with a good deal. Bet he will not answer questions but will utter something on the recorder in the interview room to cast doubt on his intent. If he is mobbed up, I bet he does less than ten years and will have a few million waiting for him when he gets out. Or so he thinks."

"Humm... You raise some good points."

Doctor Sherbahn returned to the exam room. "Hey Stu, how you feeling?"

"Like I got shot a few times."

"Good, because you were shot." The doc laughed, "Okay... the X-rays look fine. You have some hairline fractures along your left side. Take it easy for a few weeks and they should heal up fine." Holding out a slip of paper. "Pain management. You might need a little Vicodin to sleep. Otherwise, take regular Ibuprofen to help with swelling and general pain."

Chapter Twenty

Mike felt Detective Herrisch's eyes burrow into him. She sat looking between the papers Mike signed for Sgt. Noris then up at Mike. Finally she broke the silence. "I understand you were shocked with a TASER before being taken back here."

"Yep. Not my first time riding the blue lightning."

She nodded affirmatively. "You claim to be an officer. If you are, it would not be a big surprise. Back in the day, being hit with the TASER was a requirement to carry it. Not so much anymore. Seems like the generation coming out of the academy now is a bunch of snowflakes. They all get participation trophies."

"Tell me about it. I got a buddy. Works full time out in the academy. Told me about a recruit's mommy calling him on the phone to complain about how unfair the recruit was being graded on scenario tests. It was a use of force scenario, deadly force justified, and this kid wanted to do nothing more than yell at the suspect. Seriously, his mom said he felt if he yelled loud enough it would scare the bad guy into dropping the gun."

She let out a light laugh. "Sadly, I can see that happening. Got friends who do some teaching in the academy also and hear similar stories. Never about a mom calling but recruits wanting to do it their way versus standard policy."

Herrisch told a little story about a naive rookie who let a drunk driver walk home versus making the arrest. Apparently, the suspect told the kid a sob story. Five minutes after the officer drove away the drunk walked back to his car and crashed a mile down the road.

Mike countered with a similar story about a rookie stopping a suspicious looking guy in a commercial district in the early morning before stores were open. Soon after letting the guy walk away a business owner called saying his shop was broken into. The suspect had given the rookie a fake name and never thought to ask for an ID card to verify the name against.

The two cops talked for a few more minutes. War stories that stranger cops can share and instantly create a bond of friendship. Big city, small city, people are all the same and the police get to see it. Cindy smiled during a story Mike was telling, nodding her head showing she was paying attention.

Her smile and easy conversation made Mike tense up at a realization. This investigator was good. She had gotten him to open up and built a rapport. A classic essential skill used for interrogation. Make the suspect feel comfortable talking, so when the discussion turns from chit chat to police questions, the suspect feels the urge to keep talking.

Detective Radvich knew one other tenet of a good interrogation was for the officer to set the pace of the questioning, not the suspect. Seeing how he recognized her rapport building, he felt the need to change the pace of the conversation. He finished up his story, then before she could say anything he said, "I showed my ID and announced myself to the lady working the desk. Talked to your Detective Thompson on the phone yesterday. He is expecting me. So I need to ask why would they TASE me? You folks up here in Wisconsin have a sick sense of humor or something?"

"Maybe you should have come in disarmed if you wanted to turn yourself in to us."

"Turn myself in? I'm a cop, not a suspect!"

"After the events of this morning, you sure made yourself into a suspect."

Mike paused. What could have happened this morning? The lady at the front desk had looked uncomfortable when Mike had mentioned Stu Thompson. Had something happened to their officer? That desk worker had rushed out of her office behind the glass rather quickly. When the uniforms came into the lobby, the TASER was already out. Maybe she had not understood Mike, not actually seen his badge, got focused on the gun at his hip.

"Ma'am I spent all morning in the car driving here from St. Louis. I got up early, headed into the PD, checked out a squad from the motor pool, and came right here. Was only in town a few minutes when I came into your department. What happened this morning?"

The smile faded from Cindy's face. She leaned back and seemed to think for a moment. A half smile crept back to the left side of her face. The smirk of someone with a plan. "We had a shooting this morning."

"Was Detective Thompson killed?"

"Last I was told he was alive and in surgery. That could change. You feel guilty about putting him in that spot?"

Mike realized he walked into a trap. Detective Herrisch had been vague about the shooting. It was Mike who spoke Thompson's name. This was a snowball rolling out of control. After one person assumed Mike did it, they all are working on that biased assumption. When dealing with an officer down, it's not uncommon for cops to get tunnel vision. "Why would you ask if I felt guilty?"

"Let's not be coy. We both know you were involved."

"How?"

"Maybe we are putting the cart before the horse here. Can we rewind and start with everything you did today? Tell me when you got up and what you first did."

Mike realized she would not give up any details. Something major had taken place. Detective Herrisch had some skills with interrogations. She wanted Mike to give all the details, give him a chance to let out all the rope he needed to hang himself. Part of him wanted to stop talking and ask for a lawyer. The logical part of him said to recount the dull details of his morning in St. Louis and the drive to Platteville.

Hospital staff had been nice enough to get Stu a set of surgical scrubs before he walked out of the ER. The nurses had cut all his clothes off and walking out naked didn't appeal to him. His vest had worked, leaving Stu with little more than a few bruises and cracked ribs. He would be in a load of pain the next few days, but there was no medical reason to stay in the hospital overnight.

Deputy Chief Jefferson drove the way back to the department. His boss wanted Stu to make a formal identification of the person in the interview room. After hearing it was possible, Mike had come back to the police department, Stu wanted to see him. Look the other guy in the eye and show him he had not won. Stu wanted to tell the other cop he would testify. Let that crooked cop know that he would be in prison so long, by the time he got out he would need to live in an assisted living retirement home.

Walking in the rear door to the department, it amazed Stu to see how empty it was. Everyone on shift had initially responded out to the hospital. Given the shooting involved a Platteville officer, the only task the local cops did was secure the scene. Police talk about guarding the evidence. Officers and investigators from Madison and the state crime lab came to actually process the evidence.

Stu expected the cops would be back at the department doing reports about their actions and observations at the hospital. Officer Thompson would not need to fill out a report. The outside agency investigators would interview him about the shooting. The transcript from their interviews would serve as his report. Current policy was to allow two days for the mind to process the event before someone would formally interview Stu on the record.

The rear door opened into the shift briefing alcove. The alcove widened out into an open room filled with cubicles for officers to do their work at. A hallway led down the back length of the building towards the soft interview rooms and prisoner booking area. The front of the building had a hall leading to command staff office spaces and the lobby. The dispatch center was in the middle with an entrance linking both hallways.

Walking the length of the back hall, Stu could hear voices coming from the dispatch center. It was a common gathering point for officers. Getting closer, Stu realized he was hearing only two voices. One he picked up as belonging to Cindy Herrisch the other he could not place. Entering the room, he saw Sgt. Noris, the two-day shift officers and the dispatcher watching the live feed from the hard interview room.

All eyes in the room turned as Stu walked in. Everyone sat up straighter and clapped, seeing Thompson standing up walking under his own power. Sgt. Noris jumped up and walked over with his hand out. Stu took it, then Noris left hand reached out to give a combo handshake/hug. A common sign of brotherhood expressed by many officers who worked together. Stu broke his grip and stepped back away from the hug. "Sorry, ribs are cracked. It hurts to breathe. Don't need a squeeze."

"Ah... gotcha there, bro. Can't say I know what it is like to be shot." The sergeant was making a little dark humor joke about how he had shot a rapist earlier in the year. The two men were now the only currently serving cops at the department to have been involved in a shooting.

There was a few seconds of idle chatter as everyone in the room told Stu he did a good job. Then followed up by saying they were relieved to see him on his feet, minimally hurt. Stu just nodded and said thank you to each one. Once everyone had their turn, folks returned their attention to the screen hanging over the dispatcher's desk. Three flat screens held live feeds from the various cameras in the department and on the streets just outside. The two side screens showed a multiplex view of multiple cameras. On the center one was a full-screen view of Cindy in the interview room.

Stu looked at the man sitting across from Cindy. The dispatcher tapped some keys on her keyboard to bring back up the volume. Listening to the voice Stu felt confused. "Who is she talking to?"

Sgt. Noris turned to look at Stu. "Ahhh... that is Mike Radvich. They guy we were hunting all morning."

"No. No, that is not Mike."

Deputy Chief Johnson broke in. "It has been a crazy morning. Are you sure that could not be the guy?"

"Look at him. He has to be over six feet tall. Easily two hundred and fifty pounds. Mike Radvich is my size."

Picking up an unsealed evidence bag, Sgt. Noris pulled out a wallet. Opening it, he handed it over to Stu. A badge from St. Louis police was hooked to the right inside flap. On the left inside flap was an ID card listing the name Michael Radvich. After checking it over, Stu handed it to the deputy chief.

Rubbing his eyes, Jefferson asked. "This is very confusing. Who the fuck is that guy and who shot at my officer this morning?"

Stu felt weak in the knees. With no open chairs in the room, he took a step backwards so his back was leaning on the wall and lowered himself to sit on the floor. "Boss, I think that is the actual officer from St. Louis. When I talked to him on the phone, it sounded like he would not be here till today. Yet I met up with a dude last night."

"What are you saying Stu?"

"I don't know. I feel like I am living inside some bad spy novel. Two guys both saying they are Mike Radvich and we now have to figure out who is who. While also finding the person who shot me and tried to kill Bob."

Chapter Twenty-One

Sitting at the small table by the window of his hotel room, Greg was looking up the background on Officer Thompson. Limiting the search to open source records was hard. Greg did not want to log into any police databases creating a digital trail back to his credentials.

Thompson had limited social media. It might have been because he kept all the settings private. It could also mean the guy just was not active online. Greg knew plenty of cops who had accounts, but rarely used them. In modern times, not having social media could make a person look like some kind of outcast. Likewise, being a public figure causes many officers to distrust putting too much information out there.

A news article jumped out at Greg. Thompson had been involved in the arrest of a serial rapist. The suspect had murdered a few women, including Stu's girlfriend. Leaning back in his chair, Greg contemplated the little he had learned about the officer. That small town cop from the gas station mentioned Stu's girlfriend had died. His initial assessment of Stu was a small town average ability cop. Now Greg was feeling a little impressed by this officer.

This was a guy who kicked a hornet's nest and got stung. In Greg's experience, most people would do one of two things. The first knee jerk reaction for average people would be to retreat and wallow in self pity. Another impulsive reaction would have been to seek revenge, murder the killer. Thompson did not follow these paths. He got back on the case and helped get an arrest. Greg felt relieved he had not killed a brother in blue like Thompson.

Greg had not thought too much about the shoot-out at the hospital. At the time he aimed, Greg was assuming Thompson had on a vest. Few cops working in the United States go without body armor anymore. He might be a dirty cop, but he had no desire to kill a fellow officer. Greg was not an evil man. He had just made a shitty decision in a moment of weakness involving a woman. So now he was a puppet, controlled by someone who was a dangerous man.

Joey had told Greg to kill officer Thompson. Deep down, Greg knew he couldn't do it. Killing some loser criminal was one thing. Killing a cop was not a line he was ready to cross. After learning a bit more about this officer, Greg was confident he would not kill Stu.

What could he do to keep Thompson alive and still be in the good grace of the DeRege family?

Standing, Greg paced the small length of the room. He looked at himself in the bathroom mirror and paced the room some more. The pattern continued for close to twenty minutes when the sound of a siren in the distance broke the routine.

Stepping close to the window Greg moved the shades just a hair to see. Logically, he knew if the police were coming to the hotel they would not use a siren. Alerting a criminal to their approach would be an invitation to disaster. He could not help but to watch till he saw it was an ambulance.

Even knowing it was not a police car, he kept watch on the emergency vehicle. As it passed, he read the words Fire Department for the Village of some name he could not pronounce. Seeing the word fire sparked an idea with Greg. Destroy all the evidence that could be in Libertino's apartment.

During their search the night before, Greg and Stu had found little. However, they did not dig too deep. All they had found of interest was the ID and passport under Wayne Johns' name. Stu wanted to have the warrant before they opened all the drawers or moved any furniture.

After the hospital shootout, searching that apartment would likely be a forgotten task. The police would focus everyone on finding the shooter along with the health of the down cops. Unless Thompson points them toward doing that search, it was unlikely anyone would think about it. They are not vested in the case, don't know the details, so have no way to know what Stu's plan was.

That window of distraction would only last so long. Greg needed to act now before the officers looked back over Stu's notes on the case or asked him about what his next steps would be.

"Pack of Marlboro reds also, please." Greg had set a tall energy drink on the counter at the gas station. The clerk looked over her head, stepped over to the side, and reached up. Her hand came down with what Greg assumed to be the right box. It was red and had the Marlboro logo on it. He was not a smoker but had heard other people make the same request so it seemed proper.

"Anything else? Did you have gas at the pumps?"

"Nope, no gas." Spying the lighters on the counter, he snagged one. "Yeah, might need some fire also."

The clerk told him the total. Greg had an inward flitch at the cost of the cigarettes. It was a necessary evil. As he handed over the cash, she asked if he wanted a bag.

"No thanks. They fit right in my pocket."

She smiled at his response. Just an average customer. One of the hundreds she will see all day. Greg wanted her to forget him as soon as he walked away. Just in case the local cops come asking about odd customers and wanting to watch the video.

Sure, they had him on video from his visit to the police department, but he had tried to keep his head down. Same at the hospital. Never gave the cameras a direct view of his face. Now that he had changed his look, the last thing he wanted was to alert the cops to his new appearance.

Pulling his sunglasses down over his eyes Greg started the walk up to Platteville's main street. He walked instead of driving just as one more way to limit his exposure by keeping his personal car out of public view. The hotel lot was filled with cars. Many had out-of-state plates.

It was not a long walk up to Main Street, and it gave him time to think about his plan. Should he try to conceal what he was doing? Or should he not worry and just go for maximum damage?

It was a conundrum that the rational side of his brain worked out well before reaching the alley to the apartments. No matter how carefully he tried to hide this destruction of evidence someone would always assume it as foul play. Better to just go for broke and who cares if the local cops identify it as an arson.

Greg had never been part of the arson investigation squad for the Chicago PD. He had been to enough investigation conferences where investigators had presented on famous arson cases. These presentations had allowed Greg to glean just enough information for him to accomplish his mission.

His first task was to open every door and drawer in the place. If Libertino had anything hidden away Greg did not want to risk its survival because a cabinet door provided the needed protection from fire.

Next, he stood on the mattress in Libertino's bedroom up vertically. Fire grows up, so a standing mattress provides more surface area to heat the room faster.

Finally, he grabbed two cushions off the couch and took them to the kitchen. After a quick survey of the kitchen, he stood the cushions side by side on the floor in front of the pantry cabinet. Greg assumed all the cardboard boxes of food would help grow the fire quickly.

Standing in the living room, he took a mental inventory of anything else he should do before the next step in his plan. Once he took that next step, there was no coming back. As he thought, he absentmindedly looked up. A smoke detector.

Using a stool from the eating counter, Greg could reach the smoke alarm. He unplugged it from the wall and removed the battery. He did the same in the bedroom and the Libertino's little workout room.

Satisfied, Greg pulled a newspaper from the trash can. It was an ingenious little device a firefighter turned serial arsonist used out west. Balled up newspaper. Made a stack of the balls. Then lit a cigarette, placed hanging halfway out of a folded piece of paper. Last, Greg set the folded paper leaning against the stack of paper balls.

Greg put one of these arrangements in the bedroom at the base of the mattress, another in the kitchen next to the cushions and one on the couch in the living room. Assuming the cigarettes would take about ten minutes to burn down, Greg figured he had time to stroll away from the scene.

Exiting Libertino's apartment, Greg heard voices in the hallway below. He stopped, listened.

"I do not feel like going to class today."

"Hear ya on that, but kind of hard to get lab assignments done without going to the labs."

Greg could hear their footsteps going down the stairs and their voices growing distant. "I know, just there are much better things to be doing for the next two hours..."

Some days, luck was on his side. If fire worked its way up Greg figured a fire in the apartment below Libertino's might add to the damage upstairs. He just hoped the two guys who walked out were the only two living in that apartment.

As he picked the lock, he listened closely for the noise of a third roommate inside the apartment. Inching the door open, he called out, "Maintenance got a report of some electrical issues."

No response.

Walking into the living room, he again made a claim of being a maintenance person. Still no response, so he did a check of both bedrooms and the bathroom. No one else in the apartment.

Rushing, he removed the smoke alarms and looked for paper. These college kids did not get the newspaper, but they had stacks of typing paper by a printer in the one bedroom. As fast as he could, Greg stood the mattresses in both bedrooms on end and created piles of paper balls. In the living room, he again moved some couch cushions to the kitchen and made a paper ball pile.

In this apartment, he did not have time to think about what he might have missed. Greg just needed to light a cigarette and place it at each ball pile. Not knowing what else to do with it, Greg tossed the Marlboro box into their kitchen trash can. He put some paper balls in the trash along with one final lit cigarette. Walking out the door, all he could do was hope for the best. Well, actually hope for the worst, worst amount of damage possible.

On his walk up to the apartments Greg had passed a few sandwich shops. Some food sounded good. Plus, if he sat by the windows he might get to see the fire department's initial response. It would reassure him to see fire guys in action so he could gauge the damage he likely did.

Unknown to Greg, as he ordered his food the fires in both apartments were growing. Each of the little bundles of paper in Libertino's apartment burned as told the cashier what to put on his sandwich. By the time he paid, the bundles in the second-floor apartment had started to go.

In the second-floor apartment, the side-by-side bedrooms, each holding a burning mattress created a massive heat buildup. The wall between the bedroom and living room was a load-bearing wall. Part of the original 1897 construction of the building, with no fire breaks to prevent flames from traveling inside the walls from floor to floor. The second floor fire worked up to the third floor to add heat to that fire and pushed all the way up to the building's attic.

Chapter Twenty-Two

"How about this one?"

"I don't know. It is getting closer to my price range, but still this is a little more than I wanted to spend."

Sam had seen it more times than he cared to admit. A young man comes into the jewelry store with an engagement ring wishlist bigger than his budget. Sometimes their wishlist was completely unrealistic. Other times, Sam needed to figure out what was most important to find a compromise on. "Is it the size of the stone?"

"Yeah. I mean it should not be all about how big it is... but you know... I want that WOW factor."

Smiling, Sam pointed to a ring. "Will that size give you the wow you want?"

"It sure does, but I can see the price. I know I can't afford that one."

"In the back room," Sam pointed over his shoulder. "I have the exact same ring, but the clarity of the rock is much less. That stone is near perfect to the naked eye, but has flaws. When a stone is not perfect, then the cost can come down fast."

The kid's eyes got wide. Sam knew he had him on the hook. "Like how far down?"

"I got a couple to pick from, but there is one that I know is half the cost of that ring in the case."

"Can I see it?"

"Sure. Give me a second to step in the back and grab it." Sam turned and headed back into the inventory room. As he fished the storage case keys from his pocket Sam noticed a smokey smell in the air. The kids upstairs had a grill in the alley behind the store. Sam figured they must be making burgers, and a little of the odor was seeping into the storage room.

Back on the show floor, Sam set the ring on a mat for the young man to inspect. Sam could read the kid's expression. This was going to be his engagement ring. It was the moments like this Sam loved about his job. Matching a person with a dream.

The kid picked up the ring and looked it over. Twisting it in every direction, he inspected it over and over. Squinting, the kids held the diamond close to his face. Sam guessed he was looking to see how easy the imperfections were to spot. Without a magnifying glass, the average person would never notice.

Coughing, the kid set the ring down.

"So, what do you think?" Sam asked.

"I think you got yourself a sale here, mister." The kid replied with a cough.

Sam felt a tickle in his thought and let out a little cough as well. The grilling smell had found its way out to the showroom. His first instinct was someone must have left the backdoor ajar. Sam glanced over at his coworker, hoping he could get her attention to go check the door.

Before he could, the kid pointed. "Hey mister, that light fixture has some smoke coming out."

Turning, Sam saw a decorative sconce puffing smoke. The sconce was on one side of the door frame leading to the backroom. Looking at the other side of the door frame, Sam noticed the light bulb on the other sconce flicker. A wisp of smoke seeped out from between the wall and the far sconce.

Instinctively, Sam plucked the ring from the kid's hand. "Kelly... KELLY." His coworker turned to look at him. "Would you be so kind as to ring this young man up?" Stepping closer to her, he held out the ring. We seem to have an electrical issue with the lights I need to call about."

As she stepped closer to him, he leaned in to whisper in her ear. "I need you to bring him up to the front by the door and use the iPad to check him out. Don't panic, but I think there might be a small electrical fire. If the alarms go off you two can go outside and finish the sale using Wi-Fi access."

Kelly's eye got momentarily wide as she shot a glance over to the flickering light with a trail of smoke. To her credit she did not panic. "Okay."

Once she was tapping away at her iPad at a case next to the front door, Sam went back to the storage room. Sam's office was small. Just large enough to have a classic 1960s style metal desk set along the back wall. His laptop computer and a simple landline phone were all that sat on the desk. It was a small jewelry store with few employees, so Sam was the kind of owner who worked out front most of the day, then did paperwork at home on nights and weekends.

Before he had the phone handset close to his ear, Sam was punching numbers on the dial pad. It only took two rings for the other side to pick up, but that time felt like an eternity.

"Platteville 911. What is your emergency?"

"This is Sam from the jewelry shop on Main. I don't know if there is a fire here or not, but I would like the Fire Chief to stop over and look."

"Okay Sam. In case we get cut off, I would like to verify your call back number."

Sam gave the dispatcher his office line. She then asked for his cell phone number in case he had to exit the building. When prompted, Sam told the dispatcher about the flicker lights and the smoke coming from the wall fixtures. "I think it is just an electrical glitch but would like the chief here just to ease my nerves. Is there any way to get him to stop by without the embarrassment of all the red trucks?"

"Okay Sam, I am not going to put you on hold, but for the next few seconds, I am going to be talking to the fire chief. Just stay on the line for me."

"Yeah, I..." before he could finish saying he would stay on the line he could hear the Dispatcher talking to someone else.

It was muffled, but he made out. "Platteville to Fire twenty."

There was a longish pause, then came a reply. "Go ahead Platteville."

"Chief, can you head over to VanBuren Jewelry? Got a report of some flickering lights and smoke."

"Ten-Four Platteville. Can you advise, are any alarms going off?"

"Negative. Caller is still inside the store. Thinks it is just an electrical issue but wants someone to check just. Asked for a limited response for now."

"Understood. I will head over there now. If you still have him on the line, can you ask him to turn off the circuit breaker for those lights before I get there? If it is just an electrical issue, maybe we can end it before it gets worse."

"Ten-four, Chief." The dispatcher's muffled voice became clear again as she addressed Sam. "Are you still there, Sam?"

"Yes, I am."

"Good. The fire chief asked that you try to turn off the breakers for that blinking light if you know how to."

Standing up, Sam said. "Yeah, the breaker box is just outside my office. I will have to set the phone down to reach it. Give me a second to find the right one and flip it."

He set the handset next to the phone base and then went to the breaker box. Sam had inherited the store from his dad. His family had built the building and ran this store for five generations. When he took over the building, Sam remodeled both the apartments upstairs and his store front. While it was not a complete gutting of the building, the contractors did enough to upgrade the electrical service. Everything was labeled, so it was easy to find and turn off the breaker for 'wall lights'.

"Alright," Sam said after picking the receiver back up, "the breaker is off."

"Thanks. The fire chief is just pulling up outside now. He should come in the front door in a few seconds."

Sam said his thanks to the dispatcher and hung up the phone. As Sam stepped into the showroom, a man he recognized as Chief Porter walked through the front door. The kid used his finger to sign on Kelly's iPad as the chief walked past them.

"Hey Sam."

Sam nodded towards the customer. "Hi there Chief, how is it going today?"

The chief must have caught on to Sam's meaning by nodding towards the customer. He said nothing about a fire, just said, "Living the dream as always." Sam saw the chief's eye lock on the wall light. Glancing over his shoulder, Sam saw a quick wisp of smoke puff out.

"Can you come back to my office so we can talk in private?"

If the Chief was concerned, he did not show it on his face. Using the large metal clipboard in his hand, the Chief pointed towards the door to the backroom. "I will follow you."

Once they were out of earshot, Sam blurted out, "thanks for not making a big scene."

"I understand. Saw a little smoke come from that light. Did you get the breaker turned off?"

"Yes, sir."

"Just because we see smoke there, it could be some other circuit causing problems. You have anything weird going on lately, like computers turning off or popping a breaker when you use an appliance?"

"Nothing I have seen." Sam paused for a second. "Can't think of anything my employees would have mentioned."

The chief's metal clipboard was over an inch thick. Until Chief Porter opened it, Sam had not realized it was also a storage box. Porter pulled out something that looked like a kid's toy gun. As the chief pointed the gun at the wall, Sam noticed a little red laser dot. "Hum..." Turning the chief points the gun at the wall to Sam's office. "Yeah, that wall seems a skosh warm."

Sam could not help but wrinkle up his face. "Is that some fancy thermometer?"

"Used infrared technology. We have had them for a few years now." The chief paused. He seemed to be lost in thought. "Do you have access to the basement here?"

"Yeah, I own the building."

"Good. I see you got a breaker box here. Do you know if there is a box in the basement for the primary service in the building? How about the heating system?"

Sam bit his lip. It had been months since the last time he was in the basement. The last time was just to allow a plumber down to do the yearly upkeep on their boiler. "We got a boiler and three different water heaters down there. Boiler is zoned, it services the full building. A separate water heater for each apartment and then a small one for the shop. Other than that I don't know much about how it is all hooked up."

"Well, I would like to take a look down there first. If I don't see anything down there, can you let me see upstairs?"

Down in the basement, the chief pointed his laser thermometer at a few places and looked over some switch boxes. Sam was not sure what the chief was looking at or for. After about three minutes, Porter asked to be taken upstairs.

Sam showed the fire chief out to the alley and to the door leading to the stairs for the apartments. Opening the door, the smoke smell came rushing out into the hall. The chief had a worried expression which caused Sam to look up at the top of the staircase. A thick haze filled the upper landing right outside the door of the second-floor apartment.

"Fire twenty to Platteville," the chief said into the radio he had plucked off his belt. His voice was calm, but Sam noted a slight edge to it.

"Please stand by F20. About to page the fire department to your location. Got a 911 call about flames in the third-floor window and roofline."

Chapter Twenty-Three

Laying in bed, Stu was scrolling through movies and television shows trying to find something to watch. After they had verified Detective Radvich's identity, the police chief thought it best for Stu to go home and rest. Stu tried to object, but the chief made it an order.

Even if he was not happy with the chief's order, Stu understood why. Clinical research has shown after a stressful situation like a shooting, an officer's memory will have holes till the person has time to process the event. It would take a few days before Thompson could recount all the little details from the morning. Until then, it was better to allow others to process the scene and talk with witnesses.

It had been hours since the shooting, but Stu still felt wired. Physically, his body was drained, but his mind was racing, thinking about the fake Mike Radvich. What if scenarios also were playing in his head. What if he had killed the imposter cop? What if he had been hit some place besides his vest?

His streaming queue was full of action movies. The idea of watching a movie filled with shootouts was not of interest. No romance or lame comedy titles caught his attention. Stu clicked over to documentaries. He had flagged a few documentaries dealing with bodybuilding and Crossfit.

Not actually looking at the title, he clicked on a movie and it played. Sinking back into his pillow, Stu watched an array of people lifting weights and jumping up onto boxes. A narrator was saying something, but he was not actually listening. Slowly his eyes closed till the point where he was no longer watching folks lift weights.

Snapped back awake by the staccato beeps from his fire pager, Stu sat up in bed. A stabbing pain shot around his bruised ribs. Glancing at the television, Stu realized he had only been asleep a few minutes.

"This is a page for Platteville Fire." This crisp voice of a dispatcher came from the pager. "You are requested to respond to the VanBuren jewelry store on main street. Report of fire visible in the apartment above the store. Again Platteville Fire you are needed for a fire in the apartments above VanBuren Jewelry on Main street."

Standing, Stu moved to the window and pushed the curtains aside. Other homes and businesses blocked his view of the building, but Stu could see smoke coming from the area of the store. As he watched, the smoke got thicker and turned from an ashen color to black. It rose about thirty feet into the air before the wind thinned it out.

Closing his eyes, Stu stepped back, sitting at the foot of his bed, resting his head in his hands. The fatalist in him immediately figured the fire was in Bob's apartment. Way too much of a coincidence to have an attempt to kill Bob followed by his apartment burn up.

Stu was sure the fake detective or someone working with him must have set the fire. It was a brazen move for someone being hunted by the police to set a fire just two blocks from the police department.

Then again, if Bob had secrets still hidden someone might find the risk worth it.

The sound of the page had shocked him, causing his heart rate to go up. Seeing it was an actual fire and knowing it was at Bob's place pushed his heart rate up more. Each beat of his heart caused a dull pain in his ribs.

In the distance, sirens started echoing as volunteer firefighters left their homes. Knowing it was not proper to respond, Stu sat listening to the sirens. Even if there were not ethical issues of worker comp and administrative leave after a shooting, Stu felt the pain in his chest would make him useless at the scene.

Soon the sirens from the individuals heading to the firehouse were replaced by the wail of big fire engines leaving the station. Living just over a block from the firehouse Stu could make out the distinct engine exhaust noise made by one fire apparatus versus another. The primary pumper had a much higher pitch warbling tone, while the ladder truck was a baritone rumble.

Feeling pressure on his bladder, Stu went to use the bathroom. Once he finished, he stood in the hall, looking out the window at the top of the steps. It faced towards the fire like the window in his bedroom. He could not see the roof of the building, but the glow from the fire was now apparent at the base of the smoke.

Without realizing he was doing it, Stu slowly meandered down the steps. Slipped on a pair of shoes and walked down the hill to the fire station. He was about halfway there before thinking about how poor a decision it was to be seen out and about.

I can go sit in the radio room and listen to what is going on. There is no harm in that.

Then he played devil's advocate with himself.

It does not matter if you go to the scene or not. Just being at the station makes you 'involved' with the response. Off from working for the city means to be OFF.

Continuing walking in the direction of the firehouse, he made a counterpoint.

Listening to the radio traffic at the firehouse would not differ from listening to my portable radio while sitting at the coffee shop. HR can't prevent me from having a coffee.

His counterpoint must have won the internal argument as Stu walked into the firehouse and made his way back to the radio room. Turning the corner, he saw two men were already sitting at the desk that ran the length of the right wall. The desk held two computers and an older model base station radio used for dispatching. Both men were ignoring the computers as they looked out the window up main street at the smoke still rising into the air.

There were a couple of extra chairs lined up on the left wall of the room. That wall held a giant detailed map of the city, labeled with the location of each house number and a red dot for each fire hydrant. Stu picked a chair that allowed him to look between the heads of the other two men so he could see out the window as well.

Jamie Landker, one of them, must have heard Stu sit. Turing, "Officer Thompson surprised to see you here. Heard you were part of all that hubbub up at the hospital this morning," Jamie said.

The other Leigh Holding looked over his shoulder. "Rumor has it you got shot."

Both Jamie and Leigh had been on the volunteer fire department for over forty years. They were at that age where they could no longer be out pulling hose lines. Both also did not feel fully comfortable driving trucks in an emergency. So they retired from being active volunteers, but still come down to sit in the radio room when a call comes in.

Shifting uncomfortably in the chair. "Yeah, I took a few rounds."

"Can't say I know what it is like to be shot. But back in Nam, I took some shrapnel when a buddy stepped on a landmine." Jamie's right hand drifted up to his left deltoid area. "Couple of slivers of metal in my arm had me laid up in the hospital for a few weeks."

Because Jamie often had on a USMC hat or jacket Stu knew about his service. However, Jamie was not one to talk much about his time in Vietnam. This was the first time Stu heard Jamie gave any information about how he got his purple heart.

"My vest took the hit. I feel stupid that asshole got away."

Turning fully around to look Stu in the eye. "He had the drop on you, right?"

"Yeah."

"Hit you first?"

"That he did."

"Did you stand there taking fire or move to cover?"

"Got to cover."

"Were you able to return fire?"

"He kept me pinned down mostly, but I got some shots off. Made him seek cover and stop shooting at me for a few seconds."

Nodding, Jamie gave Stu a thumbs up. "Sounds like you did a damn fine job to me there kid. I seen plenty of folks freeze up and not respond. So don't get too upset that guy got away. You boys will catch him soon enough."

With that, Jamie turned back to look out the window. The conversation was over. Thompson sat to let what Jamie said sink in. Thinking about the morning caused his heart rate to go up.

Suddenly his ribs hurt and Stu grabbed the area by the pain and clasped his eyes shut.

"You okay?" Leigh was looking at Thompson.

"Yeah, I think so. Why?"

"You let out a low groan and then grabbed your chest. Started panting more than breathing."

Stu could not help but to tell a little white lie. "I must have moved wrong. My vest stopped the bullets, but the impact still cracked a few ribs. Had a moment of pain there."

Leigh looked at Stu for a few seconds. It made Thompson uncomfortable, like the old man was sizing him up. Stu thought Leigh might consider calling for an ambulance. How embarrassing would that be?

"Cracked ribs can be a real bear to deal with. Don't worry we will keep the jokes to a minimum, cuz I bet it hurts like a real son of a bitch when you laugh."

Stu had to stifle a laugh at Leigh's joke. "I appreciate it."

Slowly, Leigh turned back to look out the window. Stu caught Leigh's glance back his way. Jamie did not add to the conversation he just looked out the window. He kept his head slightly cocked, pointing his ear towards one of the radio speakers.

It took nearly twenty minutes for the fire crews to get the fire under control. It was not out, but from the radio chatter Stu could tell it would not be long before it was extinguished.

"Fire twenty to base."

Jamie slapped the push to talk button on the desk mounted microphone. "This is base. Go ahead chief."

"How many people you got down there with you?"

"There are two other people sitting here besides me."

"Whoever is down there, have them grab some bottled water from the refrigerator and fill up a cooler with ice. We got some guys up here in need of cold water."

"Roger that Chief. On their way." Jamie turned to look at Stu. "I bet you can't lift too much weight, but mind giving Leigh a hand putting bottles into the cooler?"

There were two oversized coolers on wheels kept next to a commercial refrigerator and ice maker in the firehouse's kitchen. Stu grabbed a handful of bottles and started dropping them into the blue plastic boxes. Leigh covered them over with layers of ice. After about three minutes, both coolers were full.

Leigh wheeled them out towards his personal SUV. Jamie came out of the radio room to help Leigh lift the coolers up into the back of Leigh's blue Tahoe. With the coolers loaded Leigh motioned to Thompson. "Jump in. I bet you want to see what the place looks like."

Without a word, Stu opened the passenger door and climbed up into the seat. Leigh made his way into the driver's seat and fired up the engine. The fire was just a few short blocks away, so the drive was quick. Seconds after parking, four volunteer firefighters had yanked the coolers out and were handing out waters to fellow members.

Thompson climbed out of the SUV and looked up at the damage to the building. Platteville's ladder truck still had the aerial up, pumping a stream of water into a third-floor window.

Chief Porter yelled out Thompson's name and motioned for the off-duty cop to come over.

Chapter Twenty-Four

"What are you doing here? I thought you were in the hospital."

"The rumors of my death have been greatly exaggerated." Stu tried to be humorous, but it failed.

"You got shot this morning. You need to be in bed son." Chief Porter stood in the middle of the street in his white fire coat and helmet. Like many chiefs, he was not going inside the fire so he did not put on the fire pants. He didn't need the thermal protection of the fire gear. All he needed was for people to find him in a hurry.

"My vest took all the damage."

Porter rolled his eyes. "I don't know what is more dangerous. The ego of a cop or the invulnerability of a male under thirty."

"Chief, I am just here as a citizen. Was already having a hard time sleeping when the pager went off. After listening to all the sirens, I decided to just walk on down to observe."

Chief Porter was looking up at the building, watching what the fire-fighters on the ladder were doing. Multitasking keeping aware of the scene yet also being part of a conversation. "I can't prevent a citizen from standing on the sidewalk watching what we are doing. However, I will not appreciate it if the police chief or city HR department come to bitch me out due to you being on bed rest."

Stu had to pause and think about what the Doctor had said when discharged. He could not remember bed rest as being part of the orders. Just ice the area and pain meds as needed. "Don't worry Chief, I'm okay."

"I have heard that before."

Before the chief could say anything more, Stu interrupted him. "Look Chief, there is something you need to know about this fire. I think it's linked to the reason I got shot today."

Looking Thompson right in the eye. "Young man, this had better not be pain pills talking to me. I will not tolerate any tomfoolery at my fire scene."

"No sir. No joke. I was up in the third-floor apartment last night with the guy who shot me."

Chief Porter took on a somber tone. "Wait just a second... Are you saying the guy who shot you lived up there and burned his own place up? Is this like some kind of suicide? Do we have a body up there?"

"No, not like that Chief." Stu needed to pause for a painful breath. He hoped the fire chief had not seen the flash of pain on his face. "You know that guy everyone calls Bob?"

"Yeah, the guy who walks around all day sometimes mumbling."

"He is the one who lives in the apartment on the third floor."

By the confused look on Chief Porter's face, he was not following what Stu had just said. "Wait, so Bob shot you? Wow, that guy was crazier than anyone in town thought."

"Bob did not shoot me. Bob was in the hospital after being hit by a car the other day on one of his walks."

Chief Porter looked even more confused.

"No one knew Bob's real name, and he did not have any identification. So I ran his fingerprints. Turns out, he was wanted as a suspect in a murder. A guy claiming to be a cop showed up. We looked at Bob's apartment together last night. Agreed to meet at the hospital this morning to interview Bob."

The fire chief looked up at the third-floor window, then back at Thompson. "I don't get it?"

"Sorry, chief, but I can't go into much more detail. I can say this. When I talked to Bob he told me that living here and walking around was his way of hiding in plain sight. Once people thought he was crazy, he did nothing to dissuade them."

"Okay, so do you think the guy who shot you set the fire up there?"

"The way the last few days have gone I would say it is a sure thing."

Porter rubbed his eyes. Stu could see the stress on the man's face. "Who is this guy? Why would he want to shoot you and burn that apartment?"

"Like I said I can't go into much detail. I am betting we should get the State Fire Marshal on the way here." Stu looked around but only saw a squad car parked a few blocks up Main Street doing traffic control.

The chief followed Thompsons gaze towards the parked squad car. "Okay. I will make sure the guys know to keep overhaul to a minimum. It might take a deputy fire marshal a few hours to get here. Should we try to get someone from the PD here to secure the scene for the chain of evidence custody?"

Stu fished his cell phone out from a pocket. "Let me call and talk to the shift supervisor. I have a feeling with the excitement of this morning, if you get on the radio to dispatch they will not send more officers down here. But if I take a few minutes to explain what I think is going on here, they will send someone over."

Chief Porter nodded his approval, then stepped away to talk with a firefighter looking to get his attention. Thompson took a few steps back toward the sidewalk opposite the fire to cut down on background noise from the fire engines.

"Platteville police department." The familiar voice of Angie Black came from his phone after only the second ring.

"Hi Angie this is Stu."

"Well hey Stu... I am surprised to be hearing from you. Is something wrong?"

Thompson thought about commenting how if he were in trouble, calling in on 911 would be better than the non emergency line. However, that might upset her and one thing every cop knows is to never make a dispatcher mad. "Personally, nothing is wrong. However, I could not help but to hear about the fire on Main street. Can I speak to the DC or maybe even the chief? This fire has links to what happened to me at the hospital."

"Oh... let me check on DC Jefferson. I know the chief is busy on the phone right now."

"Thanks."

"No problem. Hope you are feeling okay. Just hold for a second as I check on the DC."

The city had some generic hold music, a pair of guitars playing. Not rock, not classical, yet also not jazz. Just some noise to let people know they had not been hung up on, yet also would not be likely to offend any citizen who called in.

Deputy Chief Jefferson's voice cut the instrumental tune. "Stu, how you feeling?"

"Like I got shot a few times a few hours ago. But if you want the cliche answer, it only hurts when I laugh."

"Okay, so not telling jokes on this call, got it. Mind telling me what you think is going on."

Thompson spent a few minutes informing Jefferson about his walk through of Bob's apartment the night before. The same apartment that was now burning. Jefferson asked some pointed questions and Thompson gave direct answers.

"Sir, remember I told you Bob was telling me about working for the mafia? I feel like a lunatic raving about a conspiracy theory saying this but... I think the guy who shot me now burned the apartment to limit the connections between Bob and the Mob."

Stu heard a long hiss from Jefferson on the other side of the phone. "I get where you are going with this."

The DC paused for a second, so Stu felt the need to add some details. "After shooting up the hospital the guy must have called for backup. Bob said all his communications were via dead drops, so there needs to be someone semi-local. Our shooter has left town and whoever he called is now tying up loose ends."

"Yeah, yeah, I get that, but what exactly are you suggesting?"

"Well, sir," Stu needed to take a breath. It still hurt to breathe, so he was trying not to groan over the phone. "If someone is free, they need to come down here and start documenting this scene. The Fire Chief is calling the State Fire Marshal's office, but we both know it could be hours before they get here."

Jefferson's voice took an edge. "Are you down on the scene?"

"After hearing the page and all the sirens I walked up. Technically, I am across the street just watching what is going on."

The deputy chief sounded more disappointed than mad. "Stu, you should be home resting."

"I know sir, but the doctor said I need to walk around and move to help avoid blood clots. So taking a walk like this is just following the doctor's orders." Stu felt leaving out the part about stopping at the firehouse might be a good idea. "Also, once I realized where this fire was, I felt it was important to let the fire department know. Help them avoid destroying any evidence."

"Fine, whatever. Guess I can't fault you for being a concerned citizen out for a walk on public sidewalks. However, I find out you put any gear on and held a hose. There will be some major disciplinary action taken."

"Don't worry. Just here on the sidewalk watching and talking to the Chief."

"Great. So now for the bad news. I don't have anyone to send that way. Cindy took the real Detective Radvich to the hospital to interview Bob. We got folks in on overtime helping keep the hospital on a partial lockdown. The folks on shift are trying to run calls and yet hunting for the shooter. We all know he must be long out of town yet got to keep checking every possible nook and cranny for him."

"I already know the answer, but I could document the scene. Doc said I could not lift over fifteen to twenty pounds. Camera is less than five pounds."

"Dam it Thompson, sometimes you just don't know when to relax and let other people do something. You're a great cop, but as a supervisor, you will fail because you can't delegate to other people. It always seems you have to be the one to do anything on shift. Just so you know... you are not the only person at this department able to do CSI magic."

Stu figured if the DC thought he was insubordinate he could blame mental stress so he shot back. "You are the one who just said no one is available. By your own words, I am the only CSI in town right now with nothing to do."

The line was silent for too long. Stu felt his stomach turning. Maybe he had pushed too far this time. While Jefferson and him had a friendly rapport, the DC was still his boss.

"Let me talk to Chief Ruiz. This could be an issue with city HR and workers comp. I don't want to be the one on the hook for letting you do something that violates multiple policies."

After hanging up the phone with DC Jefferson, Thompson slowly walked up the block to the police department. Once inside the lobby, he scanned his ID card on the pad to allow him past the locked doors.

From the end of the hall, he could see a shadow in the doorframe to the chief's office. Someone was in, talking to the chief. Most likely it was Jefferson. Making his way down the hall, Stu tried to hear any conversation coming from the office.

Someone must have heard him coming. Jefferson leaned his head out towards the hallway. "Thompson, good timing. We were talking about you."

Stu was not sure if the DC's statement had a positive or negative connotation. His voice had been neutral. Were they upset he had walked up to the fire scene? Or were they happy because the fact it was Bob's apartment might have been missed till after it was too late? Stu decided to just stand in the doorway quietly and wait to see what they said next.

Chapter Twenty-Five

Lift nothing heavier than his camera. That was the order from the boss. Chief Ruiz saw how lucky they were to find out the fire was at Bob's apartment. While he was not thrilled about allowing Thompson to aid in the investigation, Chief Ruiz also acknowledged a lack of staffing resources.

"If the city HR people get upset about you taking photos on that scene I will take the blame."

Chief Ruiz was a cop's cop. He had been a member of the New York state police, working everything from patrol to investigations. Before moving to Wisconsin, he had worked his way up the ladder to a mid tier administrative rank. Ultimately, he did not have the political connections to move up to a top role like chief. Realizing he had reached his peak, he retired and moved to the Midwest where modest size cities like Platteville were eager to hire an experienced big department cop for a chief role.

The son of an immigrant Ruiz had to work for all his promotions. Officers working around him were second and third generation cops promoted because of family connections. As a boss Ruiz always remembered his roots and did his best to support officers working for him. They often described him as the kind of guy who did not stand behind his employees. He stood next to employees shoulder to shoulder.

Standing outside the burnt building snapping photos, it did not surprise Stu his chief was allowing him to help this investigation. Back in the office this chief had asked, "Even if you can physically help, what about conflict of interest issues?"

"I doubt there will be conflict issues," Stu had said to his boss. "The guy who shot must have left town right away. It took hours for this fire to happen, so he must have reported it to his superiors and they sent a clean-up crew."

Stu stood in the middle of Main street taking photos of the address number and the business name for the building. He then snapped photos showing the damage that was visible from the road.

Between photos, he thought about how the chief had smirked. "When I was out in New York, we had a case where a hitman was sent to silence a witness in the hospital. It went sideways somewhat like today did. Two days later, the witness's house burned down and we found that hitman's body in the house. His buddies double crossed him. Shot him then set the fire." Chief Ruiz paused for a second. "I know we have to be careful what we wish for, but maybe we will find the guy who shot you in that burned out apartment."

Moving to the back of the building, Stu took photos of the damage visible from the parking lot and alley. Moving inside, he thought more about his discussion with the chief. "Can't say I wish anyone dead. But can't say I would feel sorry if I found his body up in the apartment."

The Chief had cocked his head. "If you find his body in the apartment? You assume I am going to allow you to stay in the scene?"

"I mean no disrespect, Chief. You had told me about some mob cases you worked for the New York state police. Something like this you don't want to leave to chance. It might be two hours before the fire marshal gets here. I just want to go take some photos to document the scene. If the fire rekindles, we lose everything."

Rekindles happen when a fire reignites after the fire department thinks they have put it out. After a fire, firefighters will do what is called overhaul, hoping to prevent a rekindle. Investigators cringe at overhaul because it can destroy evidence. It is a chicken and the egg issue. What should happen first? Overhaul or investigation?

Investigators need to see the burn patterns to trace the path the fire took as it grew. Pull down the drywall and the patterns get lost. Wait for the fire marshal and risk the fire starting backup, which will damage the patterns. What comes first, chicken or egg?

Thompson was on the landing on the second floor. The fire had stayed inside the apartment with nothing but minor smoke damage to the hallway areas. Clicking away photos and making notes on a pad of paper. From the doorframe, he could see fire damage inside the apartment to the kitchen and in the living room. Separating the two areas was an island counter, with minor fire damage. The countertop was discolored from heat, but the wood below it was nearly pristine. The damage in the two rooms was isolated. No charring connected the bedrooms to the kitchen.

It was not definitive proof, but from the doorway Stu was sure he had indicators of arson. He held the camera to his eye, working the ring at the end of the lens to for the sharpest focus before capturing the image.

Slowly stepping into the apartment Stu turned to inspect the wall and backside of the door. The separation between the living room and kitchen fire was more distinct on this wall. Careful of where he stepped Stu took photos of the full wall and closer images showing where the burn lines ended.

Allowing the camera to hang from his neck, Thompson pulled his notepad out to make a few notes. As he wrote, his mind drifted back to the discussion with his chief.

"So what do you propose we should do while waiting for the fire marshal to get down here?"

Thompson knew after bringing up the idea of a rekindle the chief would ask what they should do. "The doc said my restriction for the next few days is to not lift more than about ten pounds. About a gallon of milk was the comparison stated on the discharge form. My camera weighs a lot less than that."

After completing the photos in the living room, Stu walked back to the first of the two bedrooms. Immediately, he saw how the melted mattress springs were not in the proper configuration. The springs and wire frame linking them were all mushed towards the headboard. If he were a gambling man, Stu would have bet money the mattress was standing on end during the fire versus laying as it should.

Scanning the room, it was a total loss. A burning mattress has more than enough heat energy to push a room over 1,200 degrees, other-wise known as flashover. He had seen many training videos showing how fast a standing mattress can kick off a flashover.

Taking photos of the first bedroom, Thompson felt he had made a conclusive case for Arson. It looked like separate fires were started in the living room and kitchen. In his mind, he imagined a third fire had been set in the bedroom. He wanted to move some debris to see better but knew he better not after the chief's chiding. Stu had some slack, best to avoid hanging himself with it.

Leaving the first bedroom, Stu made his way over to the second one. While he should have expected it, it surprised Stu to see the mattress springs again mushed up towards the headboard. Someone had set four fires in this apartment.

After taking a dozen photos in the second bedroom, Stu paused for a second. Something was not right. If Bob's apartment was the target, why set four fires in the second-floor apartment? Was it possible the person who set the fire got confused about what apartment was Bob's? Who lived in this apartment and where were they?

"Think dirty..." Thompson said to himself. Something an instructor had always said in college. Cops need to think dirty. When working a scene, think like a criminal. How would you commit the crime if you were the suspect?

A knot formed in Stu's stomach. The second-floor apartment had the feel of college student housing. Did whoever set the fire do something to the kids who lived here? There was enough debris in the bedrooms that a body could be hidden in each room. That would explain the overkill on setting four fires.

"Hey Thompson, you in there?" Chief Porter's voice came from the landing outside the apartment.

"Yeah, Chief."

"I got one of the guys who lives here on the second floor down on the street. You want to talk to him?"

The knot in Stu's stomach eased up just a little. "I still need to get photos from the third floor. Have him sit tight. Stu paused for a second. "Did he say anything about roommates? There are two bedrooms in here, both with beds."

"When I was talking to him he asked if he could text his roommate. He both sent and received a flurry of messages. I am assuming he was chatting with that roommate who must still be up on campus some place."

Breathing a sigh of relief, Stu walked out onto the landing. Thinking about how his job was to just take photos Thompson told the fire chief to have the victims wait. "It might be best to just hold off and let the fire marshal talk to them first. I would rather not muddy up the interview process."

After the chief walked back down the stairs, Stu headed up to the third floor. He was not surprised to see multiple fires had been set in Bob's apartment.

Chapter Twenty-Six

Greg took the tray with his food towards a table by the window. Sitting down, he noticed some wisps of smoke visible at the edges of the third-floor windows across the street. No one else in the restaurant nor anyone on the street seemed to notice. Then again, it is easier to notice a slight detail when looking to see something expected.

Unwrapping his sandwich, Greg forced himself to not stare up at the apartment windows. Pulling out his phone, he tapped on the icon for email and stated, glancing at one of the newsletters he got daily. Cops have the bad habit of being aware of everything around them. Greg was not actually eavesdropping, but could not help but overhear the table behind him when a woman gasped.

"There is smoke coming from that window." He did not want to turn and look, but Greg assumed she was pointing across to the apartments.

"Where?"

Her voice went up an octave. "Over there! Above the jewelry store."

"Are you sure? I don't see anything..."

"Look at the edge of the one on the right. On the third floor."

His voice took on an edge. "Oh shit you're right. But that is not coming from the third floor. Look at the window below it. The smoke is coming from that one."

Based on their conversation Greg looked up from his phone and over at the building. Sure enough, there was smoke coming from both the second and third floors.

"Should we call 911?"

The male gave a quick response that was almost chiding the lady he was with. "Apartments and commercial buildings like that are required to have fire alarm systems. I bet there are some pot heads up there smoking a bowl. If there was an actual fire, we would hear the alarm over here."

Greg could not believe his luck with what he had just heard. Human nature was to dismiss trouble. People always want to believe they are safe. Write off warning signs as something innocent to feel better. There is also a desire to not get involved. If the smoke was at their home, that guy would be on the phone in a second. However, seeing how it was someone else's place he jumped to the conclusion the building had a properly working alarm system.

Going back to his phone, Greg could hear the couple's conversation shifting to which movie they should watch later in the night. The crinkling of wrappers being balled up signaled the couple had finished their meal. From the corner of his eye, Greg saw them walk past and toss out their trash. A few seconds after, they walked past the window, heading up the sidewalk towards campus.

A positive about eating a cold sub and chips was he could eat slowly without his food getting nasty. Greg knew the DeReges would want to know how badly damaging the fire had been. He needed to sit tight for as long as possible. Slowly, he took a small bite of his sandwich while reading over the information on his phone screen.

People around him filtered out of their seats, and others replaced them. No one else seemed to notice the fire building across the street. Stealing glances, Greg noticed the puffs of smoke seemed to grow.

A commotion on the sidewalk caught his attention. A group of three people stopped outside the window. He couldn't make out the words, but their muffled voices had an excited tone. Looking out at them, he saw two of them pointing. The third was dialing on her phone.

Tracking in the direction they pointed, it amazed Greg to see flames visible coming out of the third-floor windows and by the eaves below the roofline. He had little arson investigation knowledge, but apparently had enough to get a good fire going.

The food on his plate was only half gone. Greg assumed he could continue to eat slowly and see much of the fire department's operations. Having the fire department on scene might allow him to eat slower yet. Fire trucks enthrall citizens, so a guy loitering at his table would not be out of the ordinary.

For a volunteer department, Greg thought the response time seemed to be decent. A couple of guys in their personal trucks showed up on scene before the first engine rolled up the main street. Once an engine parked, those first guys started pulling hoses and hooking to the hydrants. They were not as organized as what Greg saw with the Chicago firefighters at scenes back home, but they seemed well trained.

"Hey buddy, mind if I sit here?"

Greg flinched when a voice came from right at the edge of his table. It took him a second to realize someone was talking to him. "What?"

"You're sitting alone at a window table. I'm wondering if you mind if I take a seat here."

Greg looked at the guy, asking. The kid looked to be about twenty years old. Pimple faced, bushy hair, in jeans and a shirt with a comic book logo on it. Darting a quick glance at the other tables by the window, Greg noticed they were all full. Everyone fixated on the firefighters outside.

"Yeah, sure kid, pull up a chair." Better to be nice than to be a jerk. Folks remember people who they are upset with. Someone being normal is easy to forget all about. There was no reason to stand out in this kid's mind for weeks to come.

"Thanks," he said, plopping into a seat. Unwrapping his sub, the kid took a bite, leaving a mustard smear across his top lip. Mouth still full of food "wow I have never seen a real fire like this before. Have you?"

He wanted to ignore the kid, but again felt it better not to stand out. "As a kid, there was a house in my neighborhood that had a fire in the middle of the night. But by the time we woke up the fire crews were cleaning up and getting ready to go home."

Nodding his head, Greg wondered if the kid actually heard his response or not. He already had his phone out, snapping photos of the action. He had been worried the kid would be all chatty but turned out the kid just wanted the window seat to get better photos.

They sat in mostly silence. The kid made a few comments and asked mostly rhetorical questions. Greg offered token responses just to not seem rude. Greg finished his food and was about to leave when a civilian vehicle approached the scene.

Stu Thompson stepped out of the passage door of the SUV. An older looking man had been driving. He opened the back door and pulled a cooler out. Quickly, a couple of firefighters came to bring the cooler over closer to where they were working. A guy in a white coat and hat, Greg assumed it was the fire chief, approached Officer Thompson.

The two men stood in the middle of the road talking. Greg was stunned. What was Thompson doing here? Even with his vest on, taking a few shots like that should have him off work. Greg started to question if he had hit Thompson or not.

"Hey did you see the old guy had to pull the cooler out of the car, and the other guy just went to chitchat?"

"Huh?" The kid had said nothing for a few minutes, so it surprised Greg he had spoken up again.

"That SUV there," the kid pointed to the vehicle Thompson had been in. "Older guy was driving it. Young dude talking to the guy in the hat was in the passenger seat. When they parked, the old guy had to muscle a big cooler out of the back. You would think that someone younger and more able-bodied would do the heavy lifting."

Telling a lie. "I guess I did not notice that. I saw some firefighters hauling a cooler past, but missed seeing where it came from."

They sat in silence again for a couple of minutes then said , "Look at the way he is standing. I feel that guy might be hurt." The kid kept his eyes peeled on the window, never looking at Greg as he talked. "Maybe I was being too hard on him. I bet he did not lift that cooler because he physically could not do it."

"What makes you think that?"

"His right hand is basically glued to his left side. That guy talks with his hands. Watch how he gestures with his left. Yet whenever he moves his right hand, it quickly snaps back to his chest."

Greg watched Officer Thompson for a few seconds. Sure enough, the kid was right. "Huh... I think you are right."

Very matter of fact, the kid blurts out. "Yeah, I know I am. What I can't figure out is if he has an arm injury or a chest injury. People with hurt wrists and elbows like to hold them tight to the body. But if it hurt that bad for him I would think he would have a sling. So I am betting an injury to his chest, maybe some broken ribs."

"Mind if I ask why you noticed that? Most folks don't pick up on details like that."

For the briefest of moments, the kid turned to look at Greg. "I am a computer science major." Turning to look back out the window the kid then continued. "Working with code you have to spot small abnormalities to find bugs. So I see stuff others ignore. Also, I am working on a video game. I tend to watch people a lot so that I can add details to how characters in the game act."

When the kid sat down, Greg had assumed he was some kind of computer or engineering major. Smart people can sometimes key in on details others miss. This kid gave off that smart person without a social life vibe. Now Greg was perplexed why, if the officer was hurt, would he be standing at this fire scene?

When they were at the bar the night before, Thompson had said something about doing the volunteer firefighter thing. It dawned on Greg that Stu might have heard the call for the fire department. Knowing the address, he came out to see what was happening. He was likely telling the Fire Chief about how that had been Libertino's apartment. "Shit."

"What. Something wrong there mister?"

"No, I just realized I forgot something."

The kid was taking photos with his cell phone again. "It happens. You get caught up in the excitement like this..."

Greg stopped listening to the kid. He picked up his tray and made his way towards the garbage can by the door. Once on the sidewalk, he moved to stand behind a cluster of folks watching the firefighters from the sidewalk.

Thompson had moved away from the fire chief up onto the sidewalk right in-front of the window where Greg had been sitting. Stu was on his cell phone talking. Greg wanted to inch closer to hear the conversation. He did not trust that his new hair color would fool the other cop from up close.

When Thompson hung up the phone, he had a smile on his face. He started walking across the street and then down to the intersection. Greg was sure that Stu's direction of travel was towards the police station. The fires had been set hoping he would not have to kill the other officer. Now Greg's heart was sinking at the realization officer Thompson was going to have to be silenced.

There were far too many people around for Greg to pull his gun here and do it. Hanging back he walked the same path Stu was going. Even on the side street, there was no way Greg could get away with shooting another man.

Chapter Twenty-Seven

"Tell me what you got."

Officer Thompson was standing with Deputy Fire Marshal John Walker in the alley behind the burned out building. Marshal Walker had arrived about twenty minutes after Thompson finished up taking all his photos. Stu had walked back to the police station to download the camera. As soon as the Fire Marshal arrived, he walked back down to the scene.

"You know how you accuse me of bringing you scenes that are rather complex or crazy? Well, I fear this one will not disappoint." Stu took a few minutes to explain the details of Bob's crash, the story about being a mob hit man and the shootout at the hospital.

"First, is Dana okay? She told me you are her training officer. Was she with you at the hospital? I saw the news about the shooting. Figured she was okay because no one had contacted me yet."

Stu realized he should have said something about John's daughter as he told the story. "No, Dana and I were off regular duty. I was dealing with Bob on overtime. She is scheduled to be in tonight. With me off, she will get assigned to a different training officer. Should I have them stop by the scene when they get out on the road?"

"Yes, it would be good to see her. When her mom hears I was in town, she will ask if I saw her." John paused for a beat. "So, you are telling me this contract killer has been living under your noses. Seriously, you had no clue he was in town?"

"We all knew Bob." Stu felt he had to be defensive but worked to keep his tone of voice neutral. "He was just one of them local crazy guys. Walked around and talked to himself. I always assumed he was some rich person who decided to live off his trust fund keeping out of the limelight."

"I don't think I follow you?"

"You know, like, dude from a rich family. Got all strung out of alcohol and drugs. Got sent to rehab after embarrassing the family somehow. Instead of going back to his penthouse and party lifestyle he moved to a small town to live the simple life without a care in the world."

Marshal Walker nodded his head. "Interesting. But then it turns out the guy you think is some rich trust fund burnout is a mobster. I got to tell you this sounds like the plot from some cheesy novel."

"I could not make this up if I tried to." Stu felt a spike of pain and put his hands over his ribs.

John must have noticed Stu's moment. "You doing okay? You got a little wince of pain on your face and the way you grabbed at your chest."

"Don't worry. My vest took the real damage, but still I got some cracked ribs and bruising." Thompson took a breath as the pain subsided. "I should walk you through the scene."

"Yeah. Tell you what brother... show me the important stuff and then you head home. If I have any questions, I can always call you."

Thompson nodded his head in agreement. "Don't think I am going to argue with that." Pointing at the door. "Shall we get started?"

Walker opened the doorway to the apartments and motioned for Stu to go first. The two men made their way to the second floor landing. Once there, Thompson told Walker about noticing the separate fires in the kitchen, living room, and both bedrooms.

"Sorry if you already told me. Did this Bob guy live here on the second floor or up on the third floor?"

"Third floor was Bob's."

Walker had a camera of his own. He took a few photos and then entered the apartment. Stu watched as John took nearly identical photos of what he had taken a little bit ago.

"Wow yeah, I see what you mean by two fires in this area. Although if the fire hit flashover, there could be ways to explain patterns like this. Just playing devil's advocate here. Could there have been a kitchen fire? The room got hot enough for the curtains by the couch to light? This second fire could just be the curtains falling and setting off a dropdown fire."

Stu had not considered that possibility. However, based on what he saw in the bedrooms there was no need for devil's advocate playing. "Well, given the totality of the situation with Bob I doubt this is a cooking accident."

"Don't get upset Stu. You know how this works… we have to rule out possible causes to better zero in what we think could be the cause."

"Sure, I know. However, take a look in the bedrooms. Things like dropdown fire or ventilation push can't explain some of what you will see in there."

"Like I said I was just playing devil's advocate. I think you are right. I also think you might be a bit too close to this case. If you think the arsonist is the person who shot you, well, then you are going to be working harder to make this arson."

Closing his eyes, Thompson took a breath. Even if Deputy Marshal Walker was right, it still was not fun being chided. "I don't think the guy who shot me did this. My personal feelings are that he skipped town and now someone else is here to clean up."

Walker had the camera to his eye, taking a photo. Without turning to look at Stu, he stated. "By the tone you have it seems like you are thinking the guy who shot you might be dead. Like he messed up on his order to kill this Bob guy and paid the price for his mistake."

"It is not like I am hoping he is dead. However, that thought has crossed my mind. There is a perverse peacefulness in thinking the guy who tried to kill me might no longer be walking the Earth. On the flip side of that, it annoys me thinking we can't talk to him and find out how he found out Bob was in a crash."

John paused from taking photos. "Good point. How do you think he found out about the crash?"

Thompson had been pondering and had developed a working theory. He told John about how Bob communicated with his handlers via old school dead drops. He also gave a brief history about how Bob came over from Italy after his encounter with the DeRege family.

"So this guy walks his path everyday checking for hidden messages. He can't speak much English so has little contact with people. Thus, a local urban legend is born about the crazy guy in town. Talk about the ability to hide in plain sight." Walker points to the bedrooms. "You said there is more evidence in these rooms."

As Marshal Walker took photos in the first bedroom, Stu continued to explain his theory about how the shooter found out about Bob. "So, anyhow... I think Bob missed a dead drop. He must have been hit near the start of his route. When he missed his communication, it sent red flags out across the organization."

John was already connecting the dots. "You think this DeRege family has some cops on the payroll down in St. Louis?"

"Exactly," Stu nodded an affirmative head shake. "Bob's missed check in caused the family to alert crooked cops to find out if anyone from here in Platteville called. My call down to St. Louis got logged and next thing you know our shooter shows up in the PD lobby."

After getting a collection of photos from the first bedroom, John turned to look at Stu. "Do you think the shooter is some kind of bad cop?"

"Not sure." Stu stepped back into the main room, allowing John to exit the first bedroom and move over into the second bedroom. "He showed our dispatcher a badge to get buzzed into the PD. When I met him, he was sitting back in our comm center shooting the shit with the kid working comms that night."

"Badges are not that hard to get." John was getting photos of the second bedroom. "Heck, a crooked cop might hand a badge over to this mob family. Then later report it lost on duty after someone resists arrest. Cops lose badges in fights every so often. Gives the bad cop an excuse if some mobster is ever arrested with that cop's badge in his pocket."

"True, but this guy acted too much like a cop. Just the way he talked and held himself was very cop-like. You know what I mean?"

Walker nodded in an affirmative. "Yeah. Was the guy in like 5.11 pants or something like that also?" A popular brand of clothing for police is called 5.11 tactical. They make both duty uniforms and off duty clothing. Part of their popularity came from a line of cargo pants designed for someone like a detective. Unlike other cargo pants, they designed the pockets for holding things like spare magazines, hand-cuffs and knives.

"Dude was in the plain clothes cop tuxedo, khaki cargo pants with black polo shirt. Shirt untucked so his gun was concealed."

Snorting, Walker looked down at what he had on. Slate colored cargo pants and a red polo shirt. "Guess my colors are off."

Without missing a beat. "Nah... you're a state investigator. You boys have your own style guide." Stu then shifted back to why he thought the shooter was a cop. "When I got into our comm center he was telling a story to the dispatcher. Maybe he was a talented actor, but it sure sounded like an actual call he had been on. Heck, later we went to eat, and we swapped stories. Terms he used and the details he had just made it seem legit."

Walker motioned he was ready to walk out of the room. "Maybe he was talking about times he got arrested, but flipped the story to sound like the cop."

"That was one thought I had this morning in the hospital. I spent a lot of time looking at the ceiling in the ER, wondering what took place both last night and this morning."

The two men had made it out to the hall and were heading up the step. John Walker went from looking ahead to looking down at the carpet. The look of feeling guilty crossed his face. "Sorry Stu. I bet you don't need me Monday morning quarterbacking what took place before the fire."

"Don't worry about it." As they reached the third floor, Stu pointed. "This is, well was, Bob's apartment. It is much the same as the second floor. Multiple set points in the living room, kitchen and bedroom."

Standing in the doorframe, Stu watched as Walker's head shifted left and right. Scanning the room, the fire marshal let out a low whistle. "This was like total overkill."

"Imagine my reaction to seeing this." As they worked their way into the apartment, Stu asked. "Notice anything different about this place?"

"All the cabinets in the kitchen are open. Looks like the drawers were pulled out also." Walker stepped closer to the kitchen and put the camera to his eye. Stu could hear the shutter as John took some photos. "Looks to me like someone wanted to make sure Bob lost everything in this place. Think they were afraid he had some hidden documents listing names, dates and locations?"

"Great minds think alike."

"Did you say this all started because a car hit a pedestrian?"

"Yep. About a block from my house, as a matter of fact."

In a deadpan voice, Walker said, "Who would think a simple crash would kick up a hornet's nest like this?"

Chapter Twenty-Eight

"Hi da… err… I mean Deputy Marshal Walker."

Multiple people in the room tried and failed to hide their smirks. More than a few muffled chuckles escaped. Thompson knew that the little flub would be something folks would tease Dana about for a long time.

"No need to be all formal. Dad is just fine."

Dana's face was already red, but then darkened down an extra shade. Sgt. Noris must have felt some pity for the young officer because he verbally tossed her a bone. "Guy, I know works up in Oshkosh with his dad. My buddy is a patrol sergeant and his dad never took a promotion. Dude works with a K9. Would have to give up the dog if he became a supervisor. Even though he out ranks his old man, my buddy still calls him dad when on-duty."

Law enforcement has a family component to it. More than a few police officers have multiple generations of their family wearing a badge. Dating and marriage also add to the family dynamic of some jurisdictions.

Agent Walker had a slight red flushness growing up his neck. Not nearly as dark as his daughter, but still quite visible. "Good thing you were not a boy, like the ultrasound had made us believe. Plan was to name you John. I would have to be calling you Officer Junior then."

All the muffled chuckles turned into outright laughter. While humorous, it had not been downright funny, so the laughter abated quickly.

Deputy Chief Johnson saw an opening and took it to keep this meeting moving forward. "I realize you are just wrapping up the fire scene, but we think Dana might have caught a little break in the case. We wanted to bounce it off you before moving forward."

They were sitting in the shift briefing alcove. Thompson and deputy marshal Walker had been downloading their cameras in the officer work area when Johnson asked them to come to the alcove. As he walked towards the rear of the department, Stu saw the police chief sitting across from the real St Louis cop, Radvich, along with Sgt. Noris and rookie officer Walker.

Feeling like everyone was waiting for him, Stu said. "Ok, what did you find?"

Dana looked at Sgt. Noris.

"You figured this out. I was just riding in the passenger seat, so you go ahead. Tell them." Noris said as he made a hand gesture to all the guys sitting in the room.

"Ok, so with Thompson off Noris said I would ride with him till the FTO schedule gets figured out." Dana was looking more at the table in front of her than at the other officers in the room. "We had community service officers doing traffic for the fire, so when we started our shift, Noris said we should avoid the downtown and get out. Do real patrol work."

Pausing, Dana looked at the officers and less at the tabletop. "One of the instructors in the academy told a story about running plates in hotel parking lots and finding a stolen vehicle once, which led to catching a bank robber. I don't recall all the details but the plates did not match the car, like the car was blue but the DVM said the plates should be on a red car. Anyhow he must have then run the VIN number and found out the car was stolen. Officer went inside and talked to the clerk who remembered a guy checking in by paying cash. So they..."

Chief Ruiz interrupted the kid. "I think we all know how that story turns out. More than a few of us know cops who have had lucky breaks like that. Maybe fast-forward to the part about your possible lucky break."

"Sorry yeah... So I thought we should run the plates of cars down in our hotels. Did not find any that were stolen however had a few that piqued our interest. Down at the Motel 8 there was a car registered out of Chicago. I asked Sgt. Noris if I should maybe use the registration information to run a warrant check on the owner."

Noris added, "At shift Cindy came in and went over all the details about what we know so far about Stu getting shot. The John Doe warrant with Bob's fingerprints came out of St. Louis, but Bob had talked to Stu about the DeRege family. Which Cindy said was the Chicago mafia."

Continuing her story, Dana said. "So seeing Chicago made me do a double take. No such thing as a coincidence. When I ran the registered owner, his driving history showed an on-duty police crash."

"Do we have a photo of this guy?" Stu nearly stood up from his seat.

Chief Ruiz turned the laptop sitting in front of him so Thompson could see the screen. "Not the best photos, but a quick Google search got us a few shots."

Most of the images were group shots showing officers at an awards ceremony or newspaper photos looking across the crime scene tape at investigators processing a scene. Clicking to zoom in on an image, Stu studied it for a few seconds. "Do we have someone keeping an eye on this car?"

"Yes. We had a squad run down and park across the street at the pharmacy before Walker and Noris came back up to the PD. Why, you recognize him?" The chief tilted the laptop so he could see the screen again.

Tapping the screen right below a face. "This is the guy who shot me." Looking over at Mike Radvich. "Same guy who claimed he was you."

The St. Louis cop sat up a little taller in his chair. "What is this guy's name?"

"Greg Massana," Dana answered.

"That name does not ring a bell." Mike said. Looking at the police chief. "You should have your officers pick him up."

"I have a feeling this one might be high risk. We need to call in some of our tactical team members." Looking over at Noris. "As one of the senior SWAT members would you agree?"

"Yes Chief. He already shot at officers. I think that shows a likelihood of violence. Problem is we will probably need a search warrant to get into the room. I fear conflict of interest issues, so no judge will grant us the warrant."

Mike looked confused. "You said the FBI had taken over the hospital scene. Could they get the warrant?"

"I don't think so." Ruiz responded. "The FBI just sent a bunch of evidence techs. All civilians with no sworn agents. There are a pair of US Marshals guarding Bob. Soon as he is clear for transport, they will take him some place for agents to interview him."

With a sarcastic tone of someone who has dealt with this situation before, detective Radvich said, "Let me guess the FBI will not spend resources for this investigation until they have information proving this worth their time."

Nodding the chief said. "When I was working back east in New York, it happened all the time. We would offer the FBI a case and they would balk at it. Then, after other information came out they would swoop in and snag it. Like offering them a case on a silver platter is not enough, it needs to be on a golden platter before they will take it."

"Ok," Fire Marshal Walker said. "The FBI will wait till after they talk to this Bob guy. The US Marshals are only here to guard Bob. Can we agree this Greg guy might be a good suspect for the apartment arson?"

"That was my first thought when I found out the building was on fire." Stu absentmindedly touched his ribs. "After trying to kill me and Bob he needed to destroy any evidence Bob might have had in that apartment. It is easy to connect the dots."

Smiling, John Walker announced, "Then I guess I need to get a warrant for this guy as an arson suspect."

<hr>

"Stu, you need to think about going home. I only allowed you in today to look at that fire scene and take a few photos."

Thompson was sitting at his regular computer in the officer's work area. Nothing more than an arrangement of cubicles in a wide open rectangle shape with six computers. None of the patrol officers had their own personal desk, but each shift had an informal pecking order for who sat at which computer. "Sorry chief. Walker needed a report from me for part of his warrant application. Once I got that done, I figured I better finish downloading the photos and finish the photo log paperwork."

Grabbing a chair from the next workstation over, the police chief took a seat. "Log forms can wait. You need to rest after what took place this morning."

"Trust me, I know. My plan is to sleep for the next few days. If I get all this paperwork done now, then no one will have a reason to call and wake me up because of a missing form."

"Ok..." Chief Ruiz nodded his head. "I guess it does happen sometimes. Given the situation, I can let the sergeants know if they do case review and find something missing to just ignore it."

"It is not the sergeants I am worried about. I can imagine Cindy or someone will have to do a little follow up. Talk to neighbors or witnesses. Or if the FBI starts talking to Bob and takes this case seriously. Questions will come up, so if I can get everything nailed down on paper there is less reason to call."

Letting out a groan, the chief rubbed at his eyes. Stu could see the man was stressed. This was his retirement job. Move to a small city in the Midwest to escape the big city issues of the east coast. However, what many people forget is that crime takes place everywhere. Even cops forget criminals can live in nice towns. "You're right. Better to get it done now. Just don't be dilly dallying, hoping to somehow get involved in a warrant at that hotel room."

Thompson had not intended to try to be part of the warrant. He had however been dragging his feet a little, hoping to see Massana in cuffs in their interview room. There was something primal about the desire to see the person who wanted to kill him in a cage. "No worries, Chief. Going on a warrant service is the last thing on my mind."

"Okay there, young man. Finish up what you need to, then head home. We will do our best to make sure no one bugs you for the next few days." Pausing, the chief looked at his watch. "Okay, I need to call my wife to let her know not to hold dinner for me." Standing, he added, "If you need anything over the next few days call us. Speaking of dinner, how you sitting for food at home? I can have Linda make up a few meals."

"Wow, that is a generous offer, boss. Please don't have your wife go out her way for me like that." Stu felt a little self-conscious about the police chief offering to have his wife make food for him.

"No trouble at all. When our kids were at college, she made up these aluminum pans with meals ready to bake. Usually she made a big batch of something. Part she would cook for us, and the rest split into pans for the kids. I know it would make her feel good to help an officer out."

His voice caught for a second. Stu was not one to get emotional about something like food. It however, had been a long weekend. Heck, it had been a long few months. After Christina was killed at New Year, Stu receded back from most social gatherings. At work, he socialized with others but went home, choosing to focus on his remodeling efforts. In the days after her death, folks had made many offers to have him over for meals or to go out. After declining enough offers, soon the invites stopped coming. Something about the chief's sugges-tion of meals ready to cook hit Stu at an emotional level. "Yeah... if you are sure it will not cause her more work I would appreciate it. With my remodeling, meal prep has been a bit hard. A home cooked meal without any sawdust would be a welcome change."

"Great, I will run something over later tomorrow. Then maybe drop some other stuff off later in the week." With that, the chief walked towards his office. Turning back to the computer Stu focused on finishing up so he could head home.

Chapter Twenty-Nine

"Can I get you another beer?"

Looking at his glass seeing it was still about a quarter full Greg replied, "No rush on it. But yeah, what else do you have on tap that is a light beer?"

The waitress named off a few selections. She said one was from a local microbrewery, so Greg said he would like to try that one. She walked over to the next table and started talking to the group of guys there. Having nursed the beer in front of him for nearly an hour Greg hoped she would not rush back with his second round.

Greg sat on a bar stool alone at a high top table close to the door. After watching Stu go back to the police department, Greg had thought about going back to his hotel. He had walked back down to Main Street and watched the firefighters for a short time. People in the crowd came and went. Greg did his best to mill around, hanging towards the back of clusters of people watching the fire scene.

Thompson came back down the sidewalk with a camera bag on his shoulder. Keeping an eye on the officer, Greg saw Stu snap some photos of the outside of the building. More than once Massana figured he had a clear shot at the other cop. Thompson seemed to just have on some cargo pants and a tee-shirt. There was no way he could have a vest on. This time, if Greg shot, the bullets would rip holes into Stu's chest.

Too many people were on the sidewalks, watching still. Someone was bound to scream about a gun before he even took aim. So Greg waited, hoping an opportunity would come. It never came before Thompson disappeared into the building.

Slowly, the people lost interest in watching and disappeared off the sidewalk. Once a fire was out, there was not much to see. Firefighters loading hoses back on trucks, others milling around waiting for something to do. From past experience, Greg knew they would keep a few firefighters on scene during the early stage of the investigation. Just encase the fire was not completely out they still had a hose ready to put water on flames that might rekindle.

With fewer people on the sidewalk, Greg felt watching from inside might be better. Going back to the sub shop did not feel like a viable option. Checking the map on his phone, he saw there was a bar kitty-corner from the police station. According to the map, this bar was called Game Time. Greg assumed it would be a sport themed joint.

The location was a block away from the strip of popular college bars, so it did not surprise Greg to see a crowd of people that looked to be a mix of young and old. Crowd was not the right term. The place was not even a third full. A bar sat in the middle of the room, a few high top tables clung to the walls around the door side of the bar. On the far side, there looked to be several booths lining the back wall. Seeing the number of people eating burgers, an opening on the right wall presumably leads back to the kitchen airea.

When he entered the bar, Greg saw that from the high-top table next to the door he could see much of the front of the police department.

He could not see the main public entrance, but he had a good view of the walkway leading from the sidewalk up to the main doors. He also had a decent view of the side street where officers parked their squad cars.

If he were a betting man, Greg felt he had about a fifty-fifty chance of seeing Stu leave the police station. His vantage point was not perfect, but he was not standing out in the open drawing attention to himself. Currently, he felt he only had about twelve percent of a plan, but it was a good start. If he got lucky enough to see Thompson leave the police department, he could follow the man home. Assuming he went home on foot. Comments Thompson made the other night getting pizza lead Massana to think Stu lived walking distance to his work.

Most cops have unlisted phone numbers. Looking up Thompson's address in the phone directory online seemed unlikely. While waiting, Greg tried Google just in case, however nothing was listed. No one is completely unlisted. If allowed access to some of the Chicago police databases. Greg could have found Stu's home. However, that would leave a digital trail someone might follow back to Greg.

There were some other open source public databases he could check. There were risks using these as well. If he used them from his hotel, it minimized the trail back to him. Greg however wanted to try the direct approach first. If he could not follow Stu tonight, then he would go back to his room and try online.

"Here go, sir." The waitress said, setting a fresh beer down. Greg still had not fully finished his other beer. He pointed at the cash sitting on the table and the girl took a few bills. "I will be back with your change in a second. Sure you don't need anything else?"

"No I am fine"

"Okay... But just so you are aware we have a boneless wing special tonight." She pointed at a sign on the wall listing nightly specials for each night of the week.

"I am waiting for a buddy to pick me up. Not sure when he will get here. Would hate to order and have him be in a hurry to get going."

The server tilted her head as if considering what he had just said. "Ah, yeah guess it would suck to have to take off before the food came." She walked off only to return a minute later with his change. After setting the change on the table, she tried one more time to up-sell him. "If you change your mind on some food, just let me know. Maybe your buddy would want something... I mean everyone loves wings. Am I right?"

Greg had to admire the young lady. She was not being pushy but yet was doing her best to not take no for an answer. He stole a glance towards the kitchen area when something above the bar caught his eye. The bar made a square in the center of the room, with an island in the middle holding alcohol bottles like a back bar. Above the island, a half dozen flat screen televisions hung from the ceiling. The poles holding the TVs were covered in tee-shirts and hoodies printed with the bar's logo.

"Actually, it is getting cooler out and I forgot to bring a sweatshirt. Can I get one of the hoodies?"

The sale of a hoodie perked the girl up a bit more. "Sure can. We have them in three colors: gray, purple and black."

"Gray please,"

"Can do." She paused and looked him over. "Large the right size?"

"I'd rather a XL if you have it." He pointed at the cash still sitting on the table.

She slipped a twenty-dollar bill from under his stack of cash and turned towards the back room. "I'll be back in a jiffy," she said over her shoulder as she walked away.

Looking at the cash on the table, Greg was dumbfounded. He started out with a fifty-dollar bill on the table. After two beers and now his hoodie purchase he still had thirty-five bucks. There were some major advantages to smaller town living. Back in Chicago he would be lucky to anything left.

His beer tasted good, and it was relaxing him. By the time the girl came back, he had nearly finished the second beer. When she came back with the hoodie, she pointed at his nearly empty glass. "Can I get you one more?"

Greg gave her a smile, saying, "Yeah. That was good. Do you have anything else from that microbrew on tap here?"

"Well, we just got in a summer pilsner from them. They also have a great hefeweizen. If I were ordering something, it would be the hefeweizen, but then again I like wheat beers."

A good wheat beer was something Greg had not had in a while. The previous summer he had been on kick of mostly Belgian Ale style beers. "How is that hefeweizen? I mean, is it like real thick or like heavy?"

"No, it is not one of those beers that is all thick like tar. It is cloudy, which I think has something to do with how they filter it."

"Sounds good," Greg responded, as he pulled the hoodie on. "Set me up with one of them."

The waitress turned and scampered off to the bar. Less than a minute later, she was back with a fresh glass of beer. "Try it quick and let me know what you think."

He took a quick pull of the beer. "Yeah this is good. Thanks for the recommendation."

"You're welcome." She then reached for the stack of cash and took only a single one-dollar bill. "Because you got a shirt. This one is only a buck." After offering the kind of flirty friendly smile that gets a guy to leave larger tips, she walked over to help the people at the next table.

After what seemed like forever nursing, this beer movement on the sidewalk by the police department caught his eye. Greg had not been watching the clock, but his third beer was just over half empty. He guessed it had been nearly half an hour. A person was walking down the side street next to the parked squad cars.

Based on the size Greg thought it might be Thompson, but shadows made the face hard to see. At the corner, the person made it under the streetlamp and Greg could see clearly it was Stu Thompson.

Thompson paused, then crossed the road and walked down the sidewalk across the street from where Greg sat in the bar. Thompson was walking the road parallel to Main street heading down towards Water Street. Greg's hotel was on Water street. When they were eating pizza, Thompson said something about living walking distance to the police station in a residential neighborhood just the other side of Water Street.

Feeling his heart race, Greg took a big gulp of his beer. Reminding himself to breathe, he carefully pulled air in his nose and then slowly pushed it out his mouth. He knew what the DeRege family expected him to do. If he did not do it, the DeRege's would kill him. Taking out Thompson was a matter of kill or be killed to Greg.

Swallowing the last of the beer, he stood and sifted the money on the tabletop. After deciding on the appropriate tip amount, Greg shoved the rest into his pocket. Stepping outside, he saw Thompson was half a block away still on the sidewalk across the street. Taking slow, careful steps, Greg started following Thompson from a distance. The blonde hair and the local bar hoodie should provide enough disguise that the other cop would not recognize him. However, Greg wanted to keep his distance to make an identification that much harder.

At Water street Thompson had to stop and wait from traffic before he could cross the busy street. Greg slowed himself down also to keep their spacing. Luck helped Greg when a man walking his dog came north up Water street, then paused to cross at the corner when Greg reached it.

Keeping two steps behind the man with the dog, Greg continued to follow Thompson. After crossing Water Street, the road they walked on became noticeably narrower. The neighborhood looked to be smaller apartment buildings and duplexes. Midway down the next block, Thompson looked over his shoulder. Greg held his breath for a second worried Stu would spot him. Then Thompson stepped off the sidewalk into the roadway and crossed to be on the same side as Greg and the man with the dog.

At the next major intersection they reached, Thompson crossed the road and turned to walk, heading south. Greg looked up at the street signs. Mineral Street was the street had been on, and Broadway was the road Thompson now was heading down. The man with the dog crossed and continued on his path down Mineral street.

Standing at the corner, Greg saw Thompson walk up the driveway of a house. Continuing to watch, he saw Stu pull what must have been keys from his pocket and then open the side door to the house.

Chapter Thirty

"If you are ready to go home, I can give you a ride." Deputy Chief Jefferson was walking past for at least the tenth time. After telling the chief he would head home, it seemed they assigned DC Jefferson as a spy to make sure Thompson actually left.

"No thanks, sir. The fresh air will do me some good. A walk might burn off some of this nervous energy I have waiting for that warrant to get done."

"Your buddy Walker just left to get it signed at the judge's house now. It could be an hour before we have the SWAT guys ready to hit that door..."

Clicking the logout button on the computer, Stu stood up and nodded to his supervisor. "Don't worry boss. I got everything I can do done, so I will do as the chief said and head home."

"The offer for a ride still stands." Jefferson held up his hands to show he had a set of car keys ready.

"Nah... like I said the walk will do me some good."

"I understand." The deputy Chief slipped the keys back into his pocket. "Don't worry, the second we have him in cuffs I will call you. Let us do all the work and you just go rest up."

The fresh air on the walk home had done him wonders. Stu felt much of the stress and tension of the day ebbing. Perhaps some of it was the knowledge that in a short time, the SWAT team was about to arrest the person who created this nightmare day. A primal part of his brain wished the person they were about to arrest would resist. Perhaps even pull a gun, so the SWAT guys would shoot him.

Placing the key in his door, Thompson chided himself for wishing violence on someone else. He liked to think he was better than that. However, he knew that most men had deep down primal thoughts. Even if he never acted on such ideas, they still floated around in his recesses of his mind from time to time.

Then again, this Greg Massana was a dirty cop. The world could use a few less corrupt police officers. High-profile shootings from across the country had made police work harder in the last few years. Thinning out the number of rotten apples would be good for the profession.

Inside his kitchen, Stu kicked off his shoes. Over at the counter by the sink, he picked up a glass. Thompson's eye went back and forth between the sink faucet and a bottle of Bourbon on the shelf off to the left of the sink. Turning to look at the clock on the stove caused a sharp pain to dance across his ribs.

"Alcohol and pain meds don't mix too well. Better keep clean of the booze for the next few days." He said aloud to himself.

A full glass of water in hand, he made his way over to the remodeling zone that would become his new living room. An easy chair table and television were set up to allow some time to relax and enjoy a show. Thompson looked over the half complete construction and realized not much would get done till his ribs were healed up.

Flopping into the chair, he wondered if a trip home to his parents' house would be a good idea or not. His mom would worry and fret about his injury. As a grown man in his late twenties, he still got treated like a seven-year-old by mom.

Maybe a trip to New Orleans. Stu had a brother that worked as a television news camera person down in NOLA as the locals called it. A week or two listening to live music and eating southern comfort food might be good for Thompson's road to recovery. His brother was always asking Stu to come down and hang out. This might be the perfect time to accept the offer of hospitality.

Crack - Crack - Crack

The unmistakable sound of a cop knocking on the door echoed out from the kitchen. It was a practiced little trick of hitting high in the door's corner that made the whole door shake. The reverberation can bellow out across a whole house.

Standing up, Thompson yelled, "Yeah coming... hold one a second..."

Walking into the kitchen, Thompson stole a glance at the clock. He had only been home a few minutes, so he did not think they could have served the warrant. *Who could be knocking at the door and why?*

As he walked into the kitchen, Thompson assumed it was DC Jefferson. Stu thought the DC was going to let him listen to the SWAT raid of the hotel room. The deputy chief had seemed to want to give Stu a ride home. Maybe Chief Ruiz had some plan to keep Thompson occupied using Jefferson.

Opening the door Thompson said "Yeah... yeah what the fuck do you want?"

A gun barrel pointing at his head was not the expected answer. Startled by the weapon, Stu took a step back, allowing Massana to come into his house.

"Hey Greg... how's it going?"

It was a knee jerk reaction, but still Thompson hoped calling the other cop by his real name would put him off balance.

The crooked cop shook his gun, which Stu knew to mean to keep backing up. Taking a few steps back, he allowed the Chicago detective to come deeper into the kitchen. Once far enough in, Greg used his foot to nudge the door closed.

"So what now?"

Greg took a second to consider the question. "I guess that is up to you."

"Mind explaining how?"

"Well," Greg pointed the gun towards a kitchen chair and nodded. "I need to know what you have been told about the DeRege family and anything else Bob might have told you."

Thompson sat as instructed. "What if I don't feel like saying anything?"

"I think you will want to."

It felt more like a scene from a bad spy movie than real life. Stu grinned. "Or what you are going to torture me?"

"Not sure that I have the ability to hurt someone like that. Not in my wheelhouse. However, with a simple phone call, members of the DeRege family can be here in no time. I imagine they would not have second thoughts about making someone talk."

The image of the scene from the movie Casino where the guy had his head in a vice jumped into Thompson's head. Never in his life had

Stu thought someone would want to harm him for information. The specter of pain placed a weight on his chest, making breathing a little harder.

Greg must have noticed the fear creeping into Stu. "So you want to talk now? Or you thinking spending a few days with some professional guys sounds better?"

Thompson looked at the floor. He felt defeat. If he talked, he was dead. If he did not talk, he would still get killed, but it would take a much longer time. Closing his eyes, Stu asked, "You are going to kill me no matter what, right?"

"If it makes you feel any better, it is kill or be killed. I was told if I don't take care of you someone will take care of us both."

"So you think of this as self defense?" Stu looked up from the floor into Greg's eyes. "Kind of silly for both of us to die when only one actually NEEDS to be dead."

"You seem like a nice guy, but self preservation is what it is. I take no pleasure in doing this. My hands are tied."

A dozen thoughts raced around Stu's brain. Most some variation of the theme, this can't be happening to me. "Fine, but I want this to be quid pro quo. If I have to die, you answer questions I have about why this all went down, and I will answer your questions about Bob."

Greg stood taller. Stu's response must have taken him off guard, causing him to stiffen up. "I guess that would be fair. As a show of good faith, you can go first."

"How did a cop from Chicago beat the cops from St. Louis up here?"

"That was dumb luck I guess." Greg smirked before continuing on. "You see, a guy I know in our fingerprint section owed me a favor. Not going to bore you with the details, but had him keeping tabs on some cases the DeRege family asked me to track. One of them was a hit your Bob was part of. When you ran Bob's prints and got a hit off that cold case from St. Louis, my guy called me."

When Greg did not continue his explanation, Stu asked. "Ooookkkk... but my actual question was how did you beat them up here?"

"Ah, yeah... guess that answer was a little off on a tangent. How did I beat the St. Louis cop here... I don't know. Most likely dumb luck. When I got the call, I made arrangements to head this way that afternoon off duty. If I were a betting man your guy from St. Louis had to get a few people to give an approval to come this way. Then add that his drive was twice as long as mine. Let me guess, I was here last night. But he showed up about lunchtime today, right?"

"Yep. He showed up a few hours after you shot me."

Greg seemed to consider Stu's statement. "Interesting... your turn to answer a question. What did Bob tell you about his involvement in the DeRege operation?"

Thompson relayed the story about Bob meeting Anthony in Italy and moving to the USA. "He was the perfect hit person in that he had almost zero contact with the DeRege family. An unknown quantity to both law enforcement and to other crime syndicates. Bob was able to take on assignments that if something went wrong, there would not be any blowback to Anthony."

"Did he explain how he communicates with the DeRege family and gets paid for these missions?" Stu noticed Greg kept using the formal family name versus first names. Subservience.

Waving his index finger in a tsk tsk fashion, Stu said. "Quid pro quo, you need to answer my next question before I answer you next one."

Taking in a deep breath, Greg's face flashed with irritation. "That was the deal."

"Tell me how you got involved with this Anthony guy."

"I was a good cop," Greg stated. "Think what you want about me. I did not become a LEO looking to a guy on the take. It was a mistake I made that anyone could. Seriously, I bet a ton of other cops did what I did. It just so happened I did it so the family had a recording of me and used it to blackmail me."

Leaning back in the chair, Stu was stunned by the word 'blackmail.' "Are you saying you are not doing this for personal gain but to keep some secret?"

"Both. DeRege blackmailed me to take his bribe, so now I am stuck in his pocket. It all started when I was out with some guys at a club." As Stu listened to Greg's story about hooking up with a young lady, he felt sorry for the other cop. Dating apps on the phone like Tinder were making hookup culture mainstream. While some celebrities jump started their careers with sex tapes, Stu knew a video of a cop's hookup could be an end to their employment.

After Greg had finished his story, Stu found himself saying. "That is the kind of thing that follows you around. Not like you could have quit and taken a job some place else. Dude uploads that and tags you. Anyone doing a simple Google search will find it."

"Yep." Greg was nodding his head. "I thought about it. Got some family out on the west coast. Considered moving by them. But if that damn video was ever made public I would not pass the background check to be mall security." Sitting quietly for a moment, Greg seemed to look past Stu over towards the refrigerator. "You got any beer in there?"

"Couple of cans of cheap stuff. Can I get you one?"

"Yes, please." Stu found Gregs polite manners off putting. "Get yourself one also. Then you can tell me what you know about how this Bob and the DeRege family communicate."

Chapter Thirty-One

"Okay folks, settle down and listen up." Chief Ruiz was standing next to the sergeant's desk at the front of the briefing alcove. "You will be serving an arrest warrant on a suspected arsonist for the State Fire Marshal's office. This man is also likely the person who shot Thompson this morning."

The four officers assembled all dressed in black SWAT gear exchanged smiles. The rumor had been they would go after the shooter. Now the chief had confirmed it. Deputy Chief Jefferson stood to the side of the alcove, alternating his view between the chief and the SWAT team.

"Our suspect is a Chicago police detective. We know him to be armed and based on his actions this morning we assume he is willing to shoot other cops." The Chief paused to let that last bit sink in. "He is currently down at the Motel Eight. We have uniform officers parked across the way monitoring his car in the parking lot. Cindy went down a little bit ago and is sitting in the lobby area keeping watch for any moment."

Jefferson moved away from the wall towards the front row. He started handing out sheets of paper with photos of Greg taken off various social media sites. The chief was explaining how Dana had figured out Detective Massana was a possible suspect. Once Jefferson had passed around the photos, he moved back to leaning on the wall.

"Once we have him in custody, transport him back here for Fire Marshal Walker to integrate. DCI will process the evidence in the hotel room so we will just secure it. Once their evidence folks arrive, we will turn the room over to them." Jefferson watched as the Chief paused and scanned the faces of cops in the room. "Does anyone have questions?"

It was silent in the room. The calm before the storm. When no one seemed to want to voice a question, Jefferson stepped away from the wall again. "Let's be safe on this one guys."

There was no chatter. The SWAT cops had their game faces on as they stood and made their way outside. Jefferson followed them. Platteville's SWAT truck had started life as a delivery truck for a bakery. The deputy chief had been a sergeant when the bakery went out of business and he lobbied for the department to buy it at auction.

As Jefferson climbed into the truck, he said. "I am going to be driving you today." The officer in the driver's seat stood, then joined the other three on the bench in the back. The four SWAT cops all exchanged questioning looks. None of them seemed willing to ask, so Jefferson offered the answer to the unasked question. "If we are arresting a cop, it might look better politically if there is someone from administration on scene. I might not be kicking the door with you boys but I will be close if anything goes sideways."

The SWAT cops all made comments of approval. Agent Walker came in behind the deputy chief and had a question. "With these few people, will we have someone to watch the back of the hotel?"

DC Jefferson turned the key. He could feel the vibration as the old engine slowly turned over and roared to life. "One of the officers keeping an eye on the parking lot should be making his way around the back of the building. He will take up a position outside the target room's window. Also, when we hit the parking lot Cindy will head to the end of the hallway to block the side door. Would suck if he walked into the hallway as we are just coming into the lobby."

"You must have made these arrangements while I was out getting the judge's signature on the warrant."

Jefferson reached for the old school gear shift mounted on the steering column. There was a little sticky point in the transmission between neutral and drive. It took a few tries before he could jiggle it into place, and the whole truck lurched an inch. Jefferson could feel that Agent Walker had grabbed the back of the driver's seat for stability. "We don't do a ton of warrants here, but we do enough that we developed a system. The four guys hitting the door with you were all off duty. While dispatch was calling them to come in, I was communicating with the folks we have keeping an eye on the hotel."

"Ok. So at the briefing, when the chief talked about a car watching the parking lot and Detective Herrisch in the lobby. That means containment was already set up."

Steering the truck down the road towards the hotel Jefferson responded without looking back at Walker. "We actually did a warrant at one of the other hotels about four weeks ago. Guy out of Green Bay wanted for stabbing three people, part of some bar fight. Anyhow, one of the victims ended up dying, and the guy took off before GB police could hook him up."

"Oh yeah, I remember the alerts about the search for that guy. Any clue why he came down here?"

Not wanting to tip off Massana they were coming Jefferson did not have the lights or siren going. Stopping for a red light, he looked over his shoulder at Walker standing in the aisle between the front and rear of the truck. "His step brother is a student here at the college. We got asked to check the brother's dorm room. Kid was in his dorm and said he has not seen nor talked to the suspect. We called around to the local hotels and sure enough there is a room registered to the kid who is sitting in his dorm room."

"So we are using the same game plan that worked for that arrest?"

"Yep. All the same people in all the same roles, for the most part." Jefferson picked up the police radio microphone. Pressing the button then talking into the mic "Passing the car wash". Their radio channel was encrypted but still for a warrant they rather not use common landmarks like cross streets in communications. All the officers watching the hotel knew the car wash was just a few blocks away. Less than a minute till the SWAT team would walk into the hotel lobby. If for some unknown reason their target was listening to the police radio, he would not know this was chatter from the SWAT team heading his way.

"All I have to do is walk up to the front desk and the clerk will have a key ready for me?"

"Yep. Cindy already got a key card made for his room. Hotel management is very pro police, so they tend to help us out with very few questions asked. Once we are done, we just need to get a copy of our warrant to them for their files." Jefferson slowed up as the entrance to the parking lot drew closer. "The team will cross the lobby and hold at the room door. You just need to walk up to the desk and the clerk will hand over a key card."

Jefferson felt Walker's hand move from the backrest of the driver's seat. From the corner of his eye he could see the Fire Marshal had turned to face the men in the back of the van. "We are pulling into the parking lot now. I will get the key card, unlock the door and keep out of your way as you secure the room. Anyone have questions?"

"Yeah! The Dairy Queen is across the street…When this is done, you buying ice cream?"

Walker was quick to shoot back. "I had been planning to buy beers but if guys want ice cream who am I to judge?"

Everyone in the van shared a collective chuckle. Some last second humor to cut the tension of the situation. Jefferson was happy his people could still crack a joke, given the stress and emotion of the day.

The lurch of the van as it went up the inclined apron into the parking lot made Agent Walker grab Jefferson's seat for balance. Walked looked over his shoulder at the four SWAT cops behind him. A few seconds ago, they had shared a laugh. Now they held serious yet relaxed looks.

As the van pulled under the awning, it slowed to a stop. When Jefferson slammed the gear shift up to park, Agent Walker pulled the handle to slide open the door. After hopping down on the asphalt, Walker stepped to the side, allowing the four SWAT cops to pass him.

They paused for a slight moment, waiting for the automatic doors to slide open. Agent Walker followed the four officers into the lobby of the hotel. Scanning the lobby, Walker did not see anyone sitting on the chairs or couch off to the side by a small gas fireplace. The team made a beeline for the hallway towards the guest room while he peeled off, moving to the front desk.

Even though she was expecting them to be coming in, the girl at the desk had wide eyes. Her jaw dropped open as Walker drew closer. He saw the key card in her hand, but she made no motion to hand it over.

"I believe that is for me."

She looked to be a college student, maybe nineteen or twenty at most. Her eyes darted down to the card in her hand then up at Agent Walker. "Uh... hee...hee...here..." her hand trembled as she handed it over.

"Thanks." Walker turned to walk away, then looked back at the young clerk. "Don't worry we should be in and out in just a few minutes." She nodded and offered Agent Walker a half-hearted smile.

Making his way to the hall Walker found the team already stacked up on the door. Three were on the far side of the door, one was on the near side. The officer on the near side held a battering ram. Ready to break the door open in case the suspect had latched the deadbolt.

When he got next to the SWAT team, Walker tapped the man with the ram on the shoulder. He moved away from the wall just enough to allow Agent Walker space to hug the wall and reach the card swipe on the door handle. Walker looked at the three men on the other side of the door. All three gave a head nod. They were ready to get this arrest underway.

Reaching over Walker slipped the key card into the lock slot. In a rapid motion, he pulled it back up and then pushed the down on the handle. He felt a surge of relief when the door pushed all the way open. The dead bolt had not been engaged.

Walker could see the movement from his right. The three SWAT cops were pressing towards the open doorway. He moved his arm out of the way as the first officer stepped across the threshold. "Police search warrant!" The lead officer yelled, walking into the room. "Get down on the ground!"

The man closest to Walker dropped the unneeded battering ram and followed the other officers into the room. Walker moved from the side of the door, making his way into the hotel room. The booming voice of the lead SWAT cop repeated his yelling of "Police" and "Down on the ground!"

A hotel room is not large, so it did not surprise Walker when seconds after they rushed into the room the four officers said one after another "clear."

Turning his attention away from the rear guard post, Walker surveyed the room. No suspect.

"Fuck! where is he?" one guy blurted out.

Walker watched the first man grab the radio microphone off his chest. "Room secure. No suspect at this location. Please hold the perimeter."

Jefferson's voice came over the radio. "P2 to the TAC team. Hold tight. I will be in there in a second."

Chapter Thirty-Two

Stu was trying not to look at the gun. Greg had set it on his leg with the barrel still pointing at Thompson's belly. "When Bob was telling me about these dead drops all I could think was this sounds like some Tom Clancy novel. You know old school spy craft stuff."

Greg sat up a little stiffer in his chair. "Seems to me the DeRege doesn't read anything without lots of photos. More likely some knock off of James Bond movies."

The statement was funny, but Stu forced himself to hold a straight face. He didn't want to give Greg the satisfaction of knowing his joke was appreciated. Both men just sat looking at each other. Stu could see Greg was trying to figure out what to say next. Thompson's stomach ached thinking about every minute Greg sat silent, was a minute longer he would live.

"They never told me how they operate," Greg finally said. "It is interesting to find out more about their operation. Do you want to know something funny about the DeRege operations?"

Stu thought Greg's voice had turned conversational. It was as if he had switched over to chatting with a buddy versus interrogating a hostage. "Sure, if you know something funny." After taking a pull from the can of beer in his left hand, Greg set it down on the table. The hollow metallic clunk alerted Stu the can was empty. "Should I get you another beer?"

"If you don't mind. Have you even touched yours?"

Standing and moving towards the fridge, Stu said, "beer and my pain meds don't mix too well. A few sips is all I dare take. Don't want to vomit all over here tonight." As he reached into the fridge, Stu looked over at the other cop. "So, what is this funny thing?"

"Oh yeah, sorry... Anthony's little brother Joey lives down in Galena. That is the guy who controls your buddy Bob. Dude makes porn videos for the internet. He also manages some adult webcam performers." Stu handed Greg the fresh beer. Greg popped the top and took a deep swig from the can and set it on the table.

When the other cop did not continue the story, Stu felt the urge to prod him along. "So this Joey guy makes porno?"

"From what I hear Joey has a much better profit margin than any of the other operations the family is involved in. I mean their other operations like drugs, gambling and loans still make a major amount of money. But you know illegal operations have all the cost of people getting busted, bribes and needing to keep muscle on the payroll."

Thompson found the information oddly interesting. "You would think they would just go legit and forget the criminal stuff."

"I know." Greg sat forward in the chair. Stu watched Greg's hand move away from his gun and rested it on the beer can. "If they are bringing in that kind of cash with a small operation out here in the sticks, just think what they could do if they made videos in a real city. Way more actresses in a place like Chicago so they could make a lot more content." Greg lifted the beer to his lips. After taking a drink, he added, "I think Anthony is both too stupid and too stuck in his ways not to see the potential for a legit business. Ego of keeping the..."

The buzz of Stu's cell phone buzzing on the table top cut Greg off. The caller ID showed just a number, no name. Stu recognized the number quickly as belonging to one of the squad cars. Specifically, this one belonged to the squad car Cindy typically used.

"Who is that?"

"I am not sure..." Stu needed to think of something quick. "That might be a chick I met on Tinder."

"Oh?"

Stu thought that if he acted embarrassed Greg would drop his guard a little more. "We hooked up a few times. Mostly a friend with benefits type situation, but lately she has been getting a little more... you know... clingy."

"Wow," Greg said as the vibrating ended. "I have worked a few cases that started with a connection on Tinder and turned into some fraud. You are a brave man meeting a woman that way."

The irony of Massana commenting about meeting a woman was not lost on Thompson. Before Stu could reply, he noticed the screen on the phone light up and it vibrated again for an incoming text message. Greg reached for the phone, turning it, which forced Stu to read the text upside down. *We need to talk, call back.*

"You are not kidding that she turned clingy." Greg seemed to study the phone before adding. "How long have you been seeing her? I mean can't be all that long if you don't have her name programmed into your phone."

"A week. I think we chatted a few days on the app for a few days before we met in person at..." Before finishing the sentence Stu's land line phone rang.

Greg must not have seen the phone hanging on the wall next to the doorway to the dining room. He jumped in his chair and his head twisted quickly at the noise. "Is that her calling again?"

"Might be."

Gregs' tone went from amusement to annoyance. "Is she the type of clingy that will show up here if she can't get a hold of you?"

"She has been here before, so she could easily drop by."

Stu watched as Greg's hand left the gun, and he rubbed his eyes. It stressed the other cop about this new development, adding to the already tense night. "Answer it. Let her know you are busy and you will contact her later. Got it?"

Nodding his head as he stood up, Stu stepped over to where the phone hung on the wall. Department policy required officers to keep a landline phone. When power goes out, the cell towers don't always work, but landlines can still be used to a limited extent. Stu said a silent prayer that the department's desire to reach an officer in an emergency would save his life today. "Hello" he said into the handset.

Jefferson's voice came across the line. "Stu, I got some bad news. That Greg guy was not in his hotel room."

"Hey Tina. Yeah, what you saw on the news is real." Stu looked at Greg. Had he taken the call on his cell Stu realized Greg might have insisted on using the speakerphone function.

The other side of the phone was silent for a second before the deputy chief's voice came back. "Are you ok Stu?"

"The department sent a few guys over to keep me company for the night. Not a good time for any visitors."

"Stu, is Greg at your house right now?" Jefferson had an excited edge to his voice.

"Yep. Knowing these guys they will be here all night."

Stu could hear that Jefferson was yelling something at people around him. Then his voice came back on the line. "Sit tight. We will be there in five minutes. If you can say what is better, front door or kitchen door for us to enter?"

Greg's face was showing the call was taking too long. Stu hoped his answer would not be over the top. "Sorry Tina, I have to go. One of the guys brought some food and is cooking us a late night snack. I am being rude by ignoring them, so I will text later..."

Before anything more could be said, Thompson hung the phone up.

Greg studied him as he moved back across the room and sat back down. "So, where were we before that interruption?"

Knowing this would be over in a few minutes made Thompson feel calmer. It was still possible he would die, but that specter of death was no longer at the whim of when Greg got sick of their Q&A session. "I had just told you about the communication dead drop Bob used. Now it is my turn to ask you a question."

"Ah... Right."

Stu considered for a moment. "What are you doing with the money they give you? As in, how do you keep from anyone suspecting that you are on the take?"

Greg's face lit up. "I have a safe deposit box. Mostly, I use the money for a rainy day fund. However, sometimes I take and put some on a prepaid credit card I got." As he talked, Stu realized Greg was proud of his ability to hide his ways as a crooked cop. It was like Greg had wanted to tell someone his secret but never had the chance till now. "So, like if I take a vacation I pay for it on my normal credit card. Then later buy upgrades with money from DeRege."

Taking another drink from his beer, Greg continued. "Most guys who get caught do so because they live a lifestyle they should not. Buy a big house and a sports car. I am living modest but know how to spend on things co-workers will never notice. Keep under the radar till I get to early retirement age, then I will be gone. Move some place nice where no one knows me and will not care about what I spend money on."

"You assume this DeRege guy will allow you to move away."

Leaning back, Greg seemed to stare at his gun on the table. He ran his finger up and down the length of the weapon before looking back at Thompson. "Guys like him don't last forever. Some crook is bound to kill him someday. If not, what is he going to do? Hire an investigator to seek me out? When I say move some place nice, I mean like Honduras or Panama. A place where a guy can be a king with a decent amount of US Dollars."

Fighting the urge to look over his shoulder at the clock, Stu feigned interest in the other man's retirement plans. "Fall off the grid and there will not be much they can do to you. Smart."

"I had always thought about moving south after retirement. However, my current situation has cemented that plan." Greg tilted his head. Stu assumed Greg was looking over his shoulder to see the clock on the stove. "I need you to tell me any details Bob shared with you about any of the hits he was a part of."

Seeing how Greg had looked at the clock, Stu took the opportunity to glance at it also. The money question had burned time, but not enough for the SWAT team to make it up to Stu's house. "We only had time to talk about a few jobs he worked. Want me to start with the one in St. Louis that got us here?"

"Yeah, that would be a good place to start."

"Sure." Stu felt his voice slip a little. Worry about how the SWAT team was going to come into his kitchen sank in. Hostage rescue was not something the local police had to worry about. As the hostage, it was something Thompson was now considering. "So I don't recall the name of the victim. But he was some VIP in the family that runs St. Louis. I guess this guy did something rather personal to a DeRege member. Bob did not know what, but he was told to make it hurt. Nothing fast, as slow a death if possible. That is why a fingerprint was left. He used a knife and his glove got ripped."

"Did he do it at the guy's home or out in public?" Greg sitting forward in the chair. His right hand was back on the beer can away from the gun.

"It was not in public, so it must have been..."

BOOM, BOOM.

Two explosions echoed into the house from some place outside in the direction of the front of the house. Thompson had been expecting it, yet it still startled him. Greg, who was not expecting it, flinched so hard he knocked his half empty beer into his own lap. In reaction, Greg stood, taking a step away from the table. Sinking low in his chair, Stu kept his focus on the backdoor to his home.

Less than a second later, the doorframe splintered as the rear door flung open. The first two men in the door had weapons pointed at Massana. The first man yelled out, "Police, down on the ground!"

When Greg reached for the gun on the table, the second officer opened fire from his shotgun. The impacts of the bean bag rounds made Greg's body contort and spasm. After the fourth round hit, Greg fell sideways to the floor. Standing, Stu scooped up the gun from the table and pointed it at Greg's head.

Chapter Thirty-Three

"I hear the guys thought you were going to kill him."

Sitting in the Chief's office, Stu felt the last of the emotion of the night leach out of his body. "It tempted me. But I did not want to have to deal with any damage it might have caused to the wood floor in that part of the kitchen."

Judging by his laugh, the chief must have found Stu's try at a joke funny. "I am sure he will be happy to know that was what saved his life."

Thinking back, Stu was not actually sure why he had picked up the gun. Maybe it was just because he saw his co-workers pointing weapons at Greg and felt compelled to do the same. Regardless of the reason, Thompson helped provide cover as they placed Greg in handcuffs.

Once Greg was taken away from the scene, DC Jefferson gave Thompson a rundown of what had happened. They had parked the van two housed down and walked up via the backyards. The small window next to the back door allowed the SWAT guys to see the two men sitting at the table. The decorative frosted glass made it so they were not sure who was who. Just knowing they were sitting at the table was enough to form a plan.

Distraction from a flash bang can come in a few ways. While on television it seems they are always tossed into a house before SWAT walks in, the devices can also be useful when tossed outside. Jefferson and Walker had gone to the front of the house as the four SWAT members got set near the kitchen door. They tossed the two flash bangs towards the front of the house, hoping to draw attention away from the backdoor.

Sometimes a good plan comes together better than expected. Half drunk Greg spilling his drink in his lap took his attention further away from the rear door. It only took one hit to knock the door open, which gave the first two officers time to identify who was who. The second officer with the less than lethal bean bag shotgun decided he would not risk allowing Greg a chance to grab the gun.

"So what happens now?"

The Chief leaned forward, resting his forearms on the desk. "From what I hear, that guy is in the ER begging for witness relocation. Sounds like your buddy the fire marshal has already been on the phone to the US Marshal's service. A crooked cop would be the kind of person to have loads of dirt on this DeRege family." Stu noticed the Chief was gazing off over his shoulder. Thompson turned to see what his boss might be looking at.

A plaque on the wall, more specifically a commendation. "Ya know back east I worked a few cases that had mafia ties." Chief Ruiz was once again looking at Thompson. "That award was from a case where we got a guy into WITSEC. Did I ever tell you that story?"

"No sir."

"So our drug guys get word this pizza place is selling way more than pizzas. Truth was the food at this place kind of sucked. Anyhow, the owner had ties to high-ranking family members via his wife." As the chief explained the details of the case, Stu found the story interesting. It was a good distraction from the last few hours. Ruiz knew of a rookie cop that looked very young. They set the officer up undercover as a freshman at the local community college and eventually this kid got a job at the pizza restaurant.

"We had no clue about the mob ties till the undercover was in place. We had assumed it was just a local dealer, turned out it was much bigger. It must have been like the third or fourth week he was working when a couple of big heavy hitters came in. At our weekly debriefing, this kid is telling us how this guy was connected.

"Took us a few months to build up a solid case. When we busted him, the guy was not even in handcuffs and he asks if he could testify against his in-laws, in exchange for a new life. I guess the guy had seen some History channel show on WITSEC and decided if he ever got busted he would narc out the family."

As the chief detailed how they got this pizza shop owner into witness security, Stu's mind wandered. Part of him wanted Greg to go to jail. Another part of Thompson wished the DeRege family would make Greg disappear. Yet still, a small vengeful part of him felt sorry about Greg's story of hooking up with a girl and being blackmailed. Maybe giving the guy a break was not half bad. He also thought about Bob. The man seemed so simple, so kind, yet had murdered.

"The thing about WITSEC is not everyone gets a complete pass on their criminal charges." This revelation caused Stu to start listening to the chief again. "Our pizza shop owner gave testimony that helped in convicting four made men. He still was charged with drug trafficking and money laundering but was only given probation time. Imagine that, being moved to a new city, given a new name, and having to be stuck on house arrest."

"Bob murdered people. Do you think he will get a deal of any kind?"

Ruiz seemed puzzled by Stu's question. "I don't know. Somehow I doubt it."

"Technically, he came here illegally. Too bad we can't just deport him back home to Italy."

"That sounds like the happy ending to some movie. Too bad we live in the real world." Ruiz said. "I am sure they will work out a deal to put him in some minimum security federal prison. The kind of place filled with white-collar criminals."

"I guess that would be fair." Thompson paused. He wondered if he should voice an opinion on Officer Greg Massana or not. "Just as long as the dirty cop who shot me is not given too easy of a deal."

A smirk ran across Ruiz's face. "Don't worry too much. As much value as his testimony will have, it can't erase the sins of being a dirty cop who was willing to shoot another cop."

They talked on for another fifteen minutes, mostly Chief Ruiz telling stories about cases he worked back east. Thompson felt fatigue setting in. Eventually, the Chief must have noticed it and said, "You look spent."

"That obvious?"

"Yep." Ruiz picked up the phone on his desk. Stu saw he tapped the speed dial button for dispatch. "Hey... can't you get a patrol car to run past the PD to pick up Thompson? He needs a ride home." His voice took on a parental tone after hanging up. "I mean it this time. You head home and get some rest. Okay?"

"Don't worry. The way I feel right now, I think I might sleep the next three days."

About the Author

R. J. has been both a firefighter and Police officer. For most of his career he was a real life CSI. Outside of Public Safety work RJ is a CrossFit coach. He keeps saying someday he will move away from the Wisconsin snow but everyone who knows him will tell you that will never happen.

Want more Stu Thompson adventures click to Down Load A free Short Story

facebook.com/RJBeam

twitter.com/R_J_Beam

instagram.com/rj_beam

bookbub.com/authors/r-j-beam

amazon.com/R.-J.-Beam/e/B00B7TJFGI

tiktok.com/@rj_beam

www.ingramcontent.com/pod-product-compliance
Lightning Source LLC
Chambersburg PA
CBHW061510120726
48001CB00004B/1275